MW00593679

# The Last Will and Testament of Senhor da Silva Araújo

# The Last Will and Testament of Senhor da Silva Araújo

GERMANO ALMEIDA

*Translated from the Portuguese by*
*Sheila Faria Glaser*

A NEW DIRECTIONS BOOK

Copyright © Editorial Caminho, SA, Lisboa, 1991
English translation copyright ©2004 by Sheila Faria Glaser

Originally published as *O Testamento do Sr. Napumoceno da Silva Araújo*
by Germano Almeida.

Published by arrangement with the Chandler Crawford Agency Inc. and Dr. Ray-Gude
Mertin. Literarische Agentur, Germany.

All rights reserved. Except for brief passages quoted in a newspaper, magazine, radio,
or television review, no part of this book may be reproduced in any form or by any means,
electronic or mechanical, including photocopying and recording, or by any information
storage and retrieval system, without permission in writing from the Publisher.

Translator's acknowledgments:
Many people helped in realizing this project. First I would like to thank the MacDowell
Colony and the John Calderwood Fellowship for the residency that allowed me to finish the
translation. I would also like to thank David Knowles for his support and his friendship, and
Nancy Novogrod for her faith and her generosity. Last, I could not have completed this book
without two patient readers, my friend Mark Van de Walle, and my mother, Odete
Eugénio de Faria Glaser.

Manufactured in the United States of America
New Directions Books are printed on acid-free paper.
First published as a New Directions paperbook (NDP978) in 2004
Published simultaneously in Canada by Penguin Books Canada Limited
Design by Semadar Megged

Library of Congress Cataloging-in-Publication Data
Almeida, Germano.
[Testamento do Sr. Napumoceno da Silva Araujo. English]
The last will and testament of Senhor da Silva Araújo/by Germano Almeida; translated from
the Portuguese by Shelia Faria Glaser.
    p. cm.
ISBN 0-8112-1565-2 (alk. paper)
I. Glaser, Sheila Faria.  II. Title.
869.3'42—dc22                                2004000951

New Directions Books are published for James Laughlin
by New Directions Publishing Corporation
80 Eighth Avenue, New York 10011

# The Last Will and Testament

## of

## Senhor da Silva Araújo

## CHAPTER I

The reading of the last will and testament of Sr. Napumoceno da Silva Araújo ate up a whole afternoon. When he reached the one-hundred-and-fiftieth page, the notary admitted he was already tired and actually broke off to ask that someone bring him a glass of water. And as he sipped it, he complained that the deceased, thinking he was drafting his will, had instead written his memoirs. So Sr. Américo Fonseca offered to continue, claiming that he was used to reading aloud and at length, and the notary gratefully accepted. His voice, strong and resonant at first, even lending a certain solemnity to the proceedings, had little by little grown weaker, and not only Carlos Araújo but all the other witnesses were already straining to hear and to make sense of the murmurs emerging from his throat.

Carlos, smiling, gazed fixedly at the notary. Right from the start, when he'd seen that huge document, sealed with wax, he'd said it wasn't worth wasting everyone's time reading the whole tome, after all everybody here was practically family, or in any case among friends, and he'd proposed that they con-

sider the terms of the will known, and that in the quiet of his
home he'd read it over with due care and attention, since he
had every intention of respecting all of the dead man's wishes.
The notary, however, strongly objected to this informality, the
law is the law, and it exists to be followed and if the law calls
for the whole thing to be read, the whole thing has to be read
from beginning to end in the presence of witnesses—that was
the sole reason Srs. Américo Fonseca and Armando Lima were
present and in the end would testify with their signatures to
having attended the reading of the document in its entirety.
And, clearing his throat, he began to read at 2:45 but at 4:10
he declared he was tired and was already losing his voice. Sr.
Fonseca read until 5:20, after which Sr. Lima, smiling humbly,
asked that they let him read for just a little bit, too. And that's
how he ended up with the section that was handwritten, but in
such tiny writing that several times he stumbled over the words
and had to backtrack, and so only at around 6:30 was it possible for the witnesses to initial each page of the said will and for
the notary to arrange for it to be archived in the stack of relevant documents. And once that was done, all those present
shook the hand proferred by the discomfited Carlos, offering
their heartfelt condolences. Carlos tried to put a good face on
things and managed to gather his strength for a smile and for a
*fuck this,* and thanking everyone for their trouble said that
given the circumstances this Maria da Graça person would
have to be the one to pay the expenses, that it was only right
the witnesses not walk away empty-handed after wasting their
whole afternoon. But as he was putting on his jacket he broke
down for a moment and couldn't hold back a *the old man can
go screw himself in hell,* for which Sr. Fonseca reprimanded

him gravely, indicating, with a timid smile, that such words and rude gestures were suitable neither to the man he was and whom everyone knew, nor to the deep mourning he wore. After all the deceased had not altogether forgotten his nephew, he'd left him a little something, a wonderful place when all was said and done where he could retire in old age. So it wouldn't do to forget the respect owed a deceased uncle of whom he was in every way the heir. But almost before Sr. Fonseca could get the words out, Carlos, looking even paler for the reproof, said that he'd already wasted enough time given what he'd gotten, nodded goodbye to everyone, and ran home, mourning be damned, to change back into civilian clothes.

## CHAPTER 2

A whole new light on the life and person of the illustrious deceased—that was how Sr. Américo
Fonseca, already on his way to Lombo de Tanque,
summed up the reading of Sr. Napumoceno's will. And Sr. Armando Lima, with the rigor of a retired accountant, specified
that that was some very bright light indeed. Walking by Sr.
Fonseca's side he philosophized that no man could ever claim
to know another in all the breadth and depth of his mystery.
After all, who would ever have dreamed that Napumoceno da
Silva Araújo would be capable of taking advantage of the days
his cleaning woman came to the office to engage in a little
hanky-panky, in the corners of the room and on top of the
desk, even, ending up—and this was the best part—fathering a
child, or rather a daughter, on the desk's glass top! Letting
out a sharp guffaw, Sr. Fonseca agreed with his friend and then
began to laugh once more at the fact that it would never
have crossed their minds—and they, intimate friends of the
deceased—that he'd had a lover, much less a fruitful issue. Of
course now a lot of people would come forward to point out

resemblances, saying, You can see it in her face, they have the same watery eyes, etc., but the truth is that for twenty-five years, if anyone suspected they didn't dare say, even under their breath, that he had a child, or, rather, a daughter.

And yet, when everything was clarified and the facts established—first, on the basis of the will and sundry other papers methodically numbered and archived in various folders with indexes of dates and materials, and second, by the revelations of Dona Chica herself, who had, in the end, felt duty-bound to confide in her daughter the details of her conception—one could clearly see what could have been seen long ago: that that fine black hair was exactly the same as the deceased's, the high forehead was his to a T, and the girl's very bearing was not in a cleaning lady's genes. Without a doubt commercial blood circulated in those veins.

But even if there was more than some truth to such remarks, the fact is that throughout the twenty-five-year-long life of Maria da Graça (without the Araújo) no one had ever, out of treachery, tactlessness, or as a joke, mentioned to her a possible kinship with Sr. Napumoceno, import and export merchant, owner of wholesale warehouses, since, right after discovering her unwanted pregnancy, Dona Chica fell remorsefully and gravely ill, and left town. As she told her daughter many years later, she was caught off-guard by that difficulty not only because she'd always been convinced she was sterile but also because at the time she was already over forty, not to mention another aggravating factor, that Sr. Chenche himself was no spring chicken. Unfortunately back then there were no morning-after pills, never mind prenatal clinics or "elective terminations." So when such a misfortune befell one there was nothing to be done but to put everything in God's hands. Dona Chica went to live behind Lombo de Tanque, never coming into town, not even to do the shopping, and every month she received by a reliable messenger an envelope whose contents came, in the guise of a pension, from the firm Ramires-Araújo, Ltd. Still, it might have struck one as strange, or might have set the neighbors talking when, rather extraordinarily, on hearing over the radio the news of the passing of the esteemed merchant from this our very own marketplace, one of the most vibrant pillars of our city—Sr. Napumoceno da Silva Araújo—Dona Chica began to run around the house screaming and crying out, My protector, My god, What will become of me, etc., a display different in every way from the measured grief she had shown on the death of her Silvério who, may he rest in peace, though no model of virtue was no scoundrel either. Yet in the midst of the confusion brought on by the shock of Dona Chica having a conniption—the immediate need for water with sugar, for carrying her out to the coolness of the street, women loosening her bodice and other pieces of clothing that might impede the circulation of air as Dona Chica lay sprawled on a canvas chair— no one thought to put two and two together. And so that telling detail passed unnoticed.

Thus it was possible for Carlos Araújo, the sole nephew of the illustrious deceased, the heir in a direct line, almost, given that other nearer relations were not yet known, to mount an extravagant homage to the dearly departed, elevating his life of work and probity, his dedication to this adopted but always beloved land, his love for his people for whom no sacrifice was ever enough, his long life as an honest businessman dedicated to his city, and to conclude by recalling his exemplary behavior when it came to women: no one knew of a single love affair in the course of his nearly eighty-year-long life. For this reason, ladies and gentleman, he was right to insist in his letter of instruction that he be accompanied to his final resting place by the solemn and vibrant strains of the great Beethoven's funeral march. It seemed to Carlos the logical corollary of a life devoted to work and chastity. And for that reason, he, his only living relation, had spared no effort to satisfy this wish, just as he would do everything in his power to ensure that the firm Ramires-Araújo, Ltd., would lose nothing of the prestigious aura it had proudly acquired under his beloved and dearly missed and always-to-be-fondly-remembered uncle.

Carlos Araújo spoke these solemn words at the edge of Sr. Napumoceno's freshly dug grave and to some degree was able to prove right there and then how much he'd already gone out of his way to try and satisfy the deceased, pointing out to those present three porters bearing an enormous reel-to-reel tape player and two heavy but powerful speakers. The fact is that the fulfillment of his uncle's first request had come up against an unforeseen and almost insurmountable obstacle, for the simple reason that, at least initially, it exceeded local capacities. In truth, while it can be said that being buried to the accompaniment of a band is a Mindelo tradition and that in this regard Sr. Napumoceno had in no way departed from the traditional, the same could not be said of the music he'd selected. The obstacle emerged only after Carlos, posing one question after another, learned what that thing, a funeral march, actually was, because in the morning when he'd first read the letter, he was in no way alarmed; on the contrary, he'd even felt reassured, anything might have been expected of his uncle's oddities, at

least this was all it was. It might have occurred to him to ask to
be cremated or sunk in a skiff off the island, fancies more difficult to realize. But this way all he'd have to do is tell the bandleader that the music for his uncle's journey was simply the funeral march. The trouble started when the bandleader asked,
What's that, what's a funeral march, and Carlos, already in-
formed, replied casually that it was something by a guy named
Beethoven. We don't play that stuff, the bandleader objected.
At burials we always play *djosa quem mandób morrê*, God keep
you, whom He told to die. This funeral march thing, I've never
heard of it. Besides, it's stupid. If everyone goes with *djosa* and
no one's ever complained, why does Sr. Napumoceno come
pestering us with this other thing? For *djosa*, at your service.
For the other thing, no can do.

On this particular point the bandleader was absolutely in
the right. His musicians were already comfortable playing the
*djosa*, they played it from the church door to the cemetery, with
variations that could wring tears from the most hardened of
hearts, and, quite rightly, they didn't want to lay down their
trump card to run the risks of the unknown, wrestling with
music that probably lacked the sentiment and sorrowfulness of
the *djosa*. So it was in vain that Carlos insisted that the funeral
wouldn't be until late afternoon, they'd have practically a whole
day to rehearse, he'd supply the booze for the rehearsal, lunch
for everyone, and even a little extra pay for each man. But still
they wouldn't give in, firm and united in saying No, and Carlos
didn't relent either, this was the deceased's last wish, as the sole
and universal heir he couldn't go against it, he even threatened
to hire a special plane and send for the Municipal Band from
Praia, or for another one of their musical ensembles.

But Carlos knew that this was just talk. For Mindelo to bring in a band from outside to head up a funeral would be not only enormously and unnecessarily expensive but embarrassing, too. He didn't know what to do until the bandleader himself presented him with a solution: upon seeing the *djosa* thus rejected and dishonored, he murmured sullenly that some day a dead man would show up asking for reggae or Roberto Carlos or something like that. And there and then, through a simple association of ideas, Carlos stumbled on the solution. Roberto Carlos made him think of record players, and so he said goodbye to the bandleader, warning him that the firm Ramires-Araújo, Ltd., of which he would now be the head, would not forget this affront to its founder.

For ease of transport he substituted a tape recorder for the record player and taped 4000 feet of funeral march on a giant reel, repeating the march fourteen times. But he didn't even need that much, because they were only halfway through the seventh round when he had it turned off and began his speech.

Carlos was something of a dandy and he was conscious of the fact that the black suit enhanced his image as the dynamic entrepreneur already well known to the trade. He wanted to take advantage of the event to declare himself before the Mindelense public not only as the rightful heir of an honorable name, but also as the person who would determine the future of the old Ramires-Araújo, Ltd., which he already envisioned as the largest company in the city. And for that reason he was not against paying a lawyer he knew to write the funeral address, which he felt would symbolize the break between the company of yesteryear and what he would make of the company in the future. He began by praising the many talents of the deceased, his particular gift for business, the way in which he had single-handedly created one of the biggest commercial concerns in the city, in the whole country, even, from nothing. He spoke of his faith in numbers, of the importance he'd attributed to rigorous accounting, so much so that amounts like two cents were as religiously accounted for as any large sum. He also said that it was certainly owing to that rigor that his uncle had been able to multiply his initial capital more than a million-fold. There, at his grave, he repented for some of the grief he'd given his dear uncle, which many of those present certainly knew of. Personally Carlos felt unworthy of the good fortune that was now his, but as for his uncle, now there was a worthy and honored man, and without a doubt the crowd gathered here today signified nothing less than the ardent recognition on the part of the people of the hospitable city of Mindelo of an estimable man, who'd never allowed anyone to leave his house empty-handed, even if it was with only half a *centavo*, a bit of bread, or perhaps a cigarette. So, in this sacred place, he wanted to thank the Business Association for having made the gesture of asking its dignified associates to close up shop so that all their employees would be able to accompany to his final resting place the one who . . . etc.

And folding the speech, there and then he received sincere condolences from everyone, my heartfelt sympathies, I share your sorrow, those in attendance filing past while two men covered Sr. Napumoceno with dirt. As he accepted condolences, Carlos reflected that without a doubt it was easier and more convenient for everyone just to shake his hands right there in the cemetery, thereby avoiding the nuisance of a house full of people coming and going. Though admittedly it was the misfortune of being unable to spend the morning greeting visitors that had compelled him to do so, he'd introduced an innovation that would revolutionize the technology of mourning: setting aside a room of the house for receiving condolences and leaving a book bound in black with an appropriate pen. Thus, whoever arrived in his absence, while he was busy taping, could leave his name and message, in black and white, no mistakes. In the end he'd know who'd come and who hadn't.

Feeling tired, and wishing he could relax with a drink in hand, Carlos waited anxiously for the earth to cover his uncle so that he might head off in search of a restorative shower. Because from the moment he'd received the news and gone to his uncle's house and opened the letter that he'd found on the desk, he hadn't had a minute's rest, what with all that coming and going. Besides the music there'd been another matter that had screwed everything up and left everyone who knew the deceased open-mouthed, particularly those who'd been there when the will was read and were thus able to attest to his solid economic standing. In effect, on searching the deceased's belongings for the most appropriate clothing in which to lay him out, they'd found only one suit, and to top it off that suit was in terrible shape. The truth was, it was completely moldy; it gave off the stench of a cadaver and seemed to have spent an eternity in a sealed compartment, not only deprived of air but also subject to the activities of cockroaches and other vermin. It was not immediately possible to explain this oversight on the part of the deceased and there was no time for explanations anyway because the most pressing thing was to get past this stumbling block. But from page 168 of the will on, in the part where Sr. Napumoceno proceeded to distribute his clothes, he gave the

due explanation of this apparent absurdity, confessing not only
that he owned just that one suit but also outlining his reasons.
He said there had come a time in his life when he'd rather
lightly accepted a proposal to become partners with a firm
well-known in the business, Ramires and Ramires, Ltd., to
create Ramires-Araújo, Ltd. However, he had not taken care,
before making this decision, to obtain the necessary, verifiably
exact details of the status and stability of the Ramireses, placing his faith not only in the public view that Ramires is powerful, Ramires is solid, Ramires has capital and credit, and so on,
but also in the arrogance of the Ramireses who absolutely be-
haved in this town as if they were the kings of the castle and
not only risked large sums gambling at the Grémio Club but
were always giving dinner parties at home. And it so happened
that just after he'd made the biggest blunder of his commercial
life, he began hearing little complaints from the Ramireses
about their finances. And almost as if it were a matter of
routine, he'd embarked on the very briefest of investigations,
one that greatly alarmed him because it confirmed that the
Ramireses were navigating a sea of dismal afflictions, were
economically enfeebled, and even facing serious difficulties
coming up with the share they had promised for the new partnership. Now he was aware that he had not acted with the necessary prudence in having been content simply with the post-
ing of the share, not demanding that it be produced when the
partnership was formed, and for that reason he became
guarded, indeed apprehensive. And he concluded that he must
in no way reveal his own strong economic position, much less
boast of it. He worried that even to give vent to his fears might
end up not just hindering him but doing him actual harm.

Indeed the very opposite was necessary—to hide his material wealth from them, and present an image of austerely contained spending, to show that he was someone who lives day-to-day not on an empty stomach, of course, but without the disproportionate luxury of a daily steak either. So, as one of his first measures in this direction, he decided to eliminate the extravagance of two new suits a year, a new suit every two years was more than enough for his social needs. And after a suit had given good and effective service for the requisite two years, he would then retire it and have it sold at the Praça Estrela market.

And while on this topic it's worth noting that the Praça Estrela market merited a special mention in the will of Sr. Napumoceno, who compared it to a mini fleamarket and noted that it was there that years before he'd bought his much-envied glass-beaded lamp, coveted by everyone who visited his house, but which he left expressly as a gift to his secretly idolized daughter, Maria da Graça.

But as regards the suit, he explained that after a few years, already liberated from the terror of the Ramireses, he'd ended up preserving what seemed to him the salutary habit of purchasing a suit only every other year, given that in the end it is an unnecessary luxury in a country where you wear a suit and tie to a wedding, a funeral, and sometimes not even then. Yet, it so happened that in the period just before independence an unprecedented crime wave hit the city, adding to the uneasiness occasioned by that already grave political decision, the even greater anxiety of the vulnerability of one's person and property in a place known until then for the temperance of its customs. Providentially, this crime wave also served to clarify that he, Napumoceno, even though attentive and interested, like the good citizen he had always prided himself on being, didn't obtain the basic, incontrovertible, and sufficient data, on the question of independence, that would have led him to vote for it in good conscience. He noticed, for example, that those who wanted to be part of a Portuguese commonwealth acted with the same intolerance as those who wanted to push their adversaries into the sea. And in such a climate, no man of sense could vote in good conscience for independence, and for that reason after seeing the busts of such respected people as the great poet José Lopes or Professor Duarte Silva smashed and dragged through the city streets—as if they were not beloved native sons, but master criminals who deserved the most ignominious punishment, he decided to shut himself up at home, compose his will in peace, and wait patiently for death. However, in the middle of writing, an impulse not only spiritual but actually physical, a force whose origin was unknown to him but that seemed to guide his decisions, impelled him to make a final visit to the island of S. Nicolau, his birthplace, and in the face of this force that drove him he felt that he was nothing, and though tormented by such questions as *What will happen to my house in my absence?*, he began to prepare himself for the trip. Because he knew that people were being assaulted in broad daylight, that houses were broken into at high noon by masked men who even went so far as to rape the women. And given this state of affairs what could one expect would happen to a house that was not only isolated but uninhabited? Yet notwithstanding all that, and even at the risk of losing everything, he knew that he could not keep from doing what he had been ordered to do. And so he decided to save one thing: the suit that would be his shroud. And in the entire house he could think of only one safe place: the pantry. And so he hung the suit in the pantry, locked the door, and departed.

His choice of the pantry as a closet only made sense after it became clear that in fact the pantry was practically inviolable. Because, for some reason that Sr. Napumoceno did not explain in his will, the pantry, which had no opening to the outside, was sealed with a thick door made of pitch-pine, reinforced by two bars of steel, nailed crosswise. It was unquestionably a secure room, and there Sr. Napumoceno stored his suit. He did not explain why only the suit merited the honor of the pantry and not his other belongings of greater value, such as, for example, the famous lamp. He said only that he was already known to be an eccentric who acquired a new suit every two years, he himself having adopted this eccentricity for the convenience it brought him, because given his excessive height and thinness he could not find ready-to-wear clothing in the local market, and he didn't want to run the risk of breaking with a whole philosophy of life that had taken him years to develop. It must be said, however, that in truth, Sr. Napumoceno's suits were still considered new when they went to the Praça Estrela market for the simple reason that they only saw the light of day for the feast of Corpus Christi, the festival of St. John, and at Christmas and New Year's, when he made the obligatory rounds, whether to pay compliments to those nearest and dearest or to the Governor. Other than that, only at a funeral or a reception.

However, following his return from S. Nicolau, he was in despair. Because for some reason that up until the last page of his will he had not yet hit upon, he had, before leaving,

carefully closed up the house, even padlocked the door, but
through an unpardonable oversight left a tap running. And
when he came back, the house still showed signs of the flood-
ing—large stains on the well-polished floor, little puddles here
and there. And so he was unable to enjoy the tranquil
satisfaction of finding his things were perfectly safe because he
immediately had to arrange for the return of Dona Eduarda, to
turn the house upside down and clean it from top to bottom.
And only after several days had gone by did he remember the
pantry. He found it still full of water, the already rotten sacks
of beans and corn and potatoes practically bobbing in it, a nau-
seating odor suffocating the room, the suit hanging there
smelling as if it had just come out of a coffin. After the initial
shock, he had conceded that with luck, sun, a brush, and some
benzene, the suit would return to a more-or-less reasonable
condition and Dona Eduarda certainly tried. But it was all in
vain because when, already despairing of even diminishing
much less eliminating the smell of rotten potatoes and beans
that emanated from the suit, she had suggested an immersion
in boiling water with lye, Sr. Napumoceno objected to this
ridiculous idea, saying peremptorily that he would never as-
sume responsibility for putting a lined suit of the purest English cheviot in soapy water.

He allowed, however, that if his body came to long for the
grave before the two years were up—and there were still 18
months to go—there might be some difficulty in dressing his
corpse. But he trusted that someone would figure out how to
overcome that difficulty, just as he was overcoming the lack of a
suit by falling ill each time its use seemed indispensable.

And in truth Carlos did figure out how to overcome that

difficulty. He was granted a special favor thanks to Dona Eduarda who—having managed Sr. Napumoceno's house and office since Dona Chica's retirement—knew all the people who had acquired her employer's suits second-hand, because, following his particular instructions, she'd kept a ledger with the full names and addresses of all those who received this blessing. Thus, hardly had the hitch with the suit been discovered than Carlos said, Don't even think about wasting time looking in stores, and took immediate steps to locate the last buyer, ordering that whatever price necessary be offered. But unfortunately the last buyer had headed for the islands in search of better luck, taking the suit with him. They were only able to get a hold of the suit that had been sold eight years before, because the two subsequent buyers had already died. Happily the man from eight years ago had taken great care of the suit and when it was explained that Sr. Napumoceno risked being buried in shirtsleeves, he saw it was a case of force majeure, and though it meant relinquishing his own shroud, gave it up at cost. And so the suit was quickly ferreted out of the trunk, shaken out of mothballs and taken home again, where Dona Eduarda, interrupting her inconsolable crying at the foot of the bed, spent two hours brushing, scrubbing, and ironing, until she considered it not only presentable but also free of that old suitcase smell, as she'd called it, sobbing, the minute she'd held the suit in her hands. Even Carlos, who was returning from his taping, spared no praise when he saw the service Dona Eduarda had just rendered, saying that frankly the suit was tiptop, worthy of the most demanding dead man, and that she could count on an extra bonus once the commotion of the funeral was over. And he put a rush on dressing the deceased be-

cause though the house was already full of people there was no
sign of the body, no one to whom to give one's condolences,
and even the undertaker when he arrived with the beautiful
coffin in polished mahogany with silver handles had to prop it
up by the back door because the dead man wasn't even washed
much less dressed. I charge by the hour, he warned, and sat behind the wheel, waiting. Seeing him sitting there smoking
lazily, Carlos, who knew the price of each hour, tried to speed
things up. Washed and shaved, Sr. Napumoceno was then
dressed and shod. Dona Eduarda insisted on helping to put on
his jacket. For the last time, she said, and adjusted the knot of
his tie, which was off to one side. And placed in the coffin and
duly arranged on some air-freshening tablets, Sr. Napumoceno
entered the living room preceded by four enormous wax tapers
and was positioned on two chairs. Carlos had thought at first
of putting a bier on top of the long dining room table, but
ended up realizing that Sr. Napumoceno would be up too high,
thereby forcing people to look at him with heads raised, which
would result in a certain disregard for the rules of decorum demanded by the dead. Thus he had opted to have the coffin
placed on chairs so that heads could be kept bent, and when Sr.
Napumoceno entered the room the murmuring and whisper-
ing ceased and all those present got up and approached the
heir. The reel forgotten in his hand, Carlos hugged everyone
with care, though he was still worried. Because there was no
guarantee he'd be able to get a powerful tape player, his was
feeble, he couldn't see it making the air tremble with the
solemn chords of the funeral march. What a crazy idea of the
old man's, he thought. He was always loopy—here's the proof.

Installed on the chairs, Sr. Napumoceno received the last

respects of his fellow-countrymen and colleagues. The heads of the Business Association had come in full force: it had already been announced that the president had requested that his esteemed associates close up shop from 4:00 to 6:00 so that everyone could pay their last respects to their illustrious compatriot who for more than forty years had given his utmost on behalf of the development of the city that had adopted him but which he had treated like the most beloved of mothers.

The burial of Sr. Napumoceno was grand—due not only to the presence of an official delegation that had arrived specially from Praia for the ceremony, but also to the quantity of private cars and taxis in the funeral cortège. Coincidentally the large hearse belonging to the Mindelo Funerary Agency had just returned from Lisbon following repairs so extensive that it looked as good as new, one might even say that Sr. Napumoceno was the first to take it for a spin. Painted dark blue and completely renovated inside, with its engine tuned and its original carburetor, the enormous vehicle lent the ceremony a silent dignity that allowed for the unimpeded expression of the enormous reel-to-reel tape player, which Carlos had decided, finally, to have transported on the backs of men placed judiciously behind him.

And after the customary five days had passed, which he spent getting things at the office in order and settling those matters he deemed truly urgent, Carlos, in heavy mourning and carrying a black leather briefcase, headed for the notary's office for the formal and solemn reading of the last will and testament of Sr. Napumoceno da Silva Araújo. And in the presence of two witnesses, the notary certified that this was the same envelope he had sealed with wax ten years before, or to be more exact on November 30, 1974, a day on which at the request of the *de cujus* he had gone to the residence of same to approve his will. And he also certified in a separate document that the aforesaid envelope showed no signs of tampering and that the wax seals placed on same were in perfect condition. And then he proceeded to open the aforesaid envelope and verified that the will was written on 387 pieces of ruled foolscap, the first 379 pages were typewritten and the rest handwritten in indelible ink.

## CHAPTER 3

*Y*ou would have thought that a man as meticulous as Sr. Napumoceno would explain at the very beginning of his will and in great detail the reasons that had led him to bequeath his nephew—considered by the entire city to be his sole and rightful heir—only that old heap, Mato Inglês, which, though in total disrepair, he guaranteed would one day be worth several thousand *contos de reis*. But to Carlos, even in that regard, the greedy old devil had shown himself to be a teller of tall tales. First there was the whole story of the will that was supposedly written ten years before he died and then all that talk about the suit. Somewhere in this big house a suit is hidden, Carlos said to Graça a while later, after the hurt of being passed over had waned. Or else the old man was completely gaga. Because, look, if the will really is from 1974, and we know for a fact that he died in '84, that means that from '74 to '84, and even allowing for one suit every two years, he would still have had another five. So . . .

But not even Dona Eduarda could explain why there was no suit, which prompted Graça to suggest that naturally the old man considered himself dead in 1974, and after that had given no further thought to his wardrobe.

But what really pissed Carlos off was the fact that the old goat (such names directed at a dead man made Graça giggle) had urged him to stick to serious and productive work, to follow the example either of himself, Napumoceno, or of other town notables who, in keeping with the sound principles of labor, had not only amassed a substantial nest egg, but also earned the respect, the consideration, and even the envy of the city. He asked that Carlos pay special attention to those aspects linked to personal orderliness and discipline, and told him that however tenacious and hardworking a man is, he is worth nothing if he is not orderly and disciplined.

And in fact, what immediately impressed everyone who'd heard his will read was Sr. Napumoceno's extremely methodical and tidy mind. For example, in the section relating to his property, he provided an extensive, meticulous, and rigorous inventory of everything he owned, movables and immovables, justifying every penny of his holdings, explaining that if they were not greater it was not only because disquieting world developments make it impossible to be absolutely certain of the worth of his patrimony, but also because his gray hairs had shown him that there are things other than riches worth pursuing with equal tenacity. On the other hand, he enumerated, in order of value, everything he thought might be worth something, not forgetting, even, the two old carpets that were no longer used and already in storage and the three wooden ladders that could be found above the entrance to the pantry, one of them missing five steps, the others unfortunately requiring more significant repairs, none of which, however, diminished their relative value. He also mentioned a cardboard box on top of the wardrobe that contained three pairs of shoes (almost new) that he'd brought back from Lisbon on his last trip, all of which had one drawback, they rubbed against a corn he'd gotten while working as an errand boy for Miller & Corys. He placed the value of the ladders at 800 *escudos*, and the shoes could easily fetch 160 a pair. And so, sum by sum, adding in the value of the clothing, books, ornaments, jewels, and other smaller items, Sr. Napumoceno estimated that his fortune reached the sum total of 67,380,547 *escudos* and 70 *centavos*.

He said, however, that before delving into the distribution of his belongings, he considered it necessary to explain certain parts of his life, the steps that were most significant in my becoming a man and that in one way or another came to influence my destiny. Nor is it unfitting that I begin by speaking of my nephew Carlos Araújo because notwithstanding the fact that I am the progenitor of a beautiful girl who has already turned 15, nothing in principle would stop me from leaving him a large piece of the pie. He's already rubbing his hands together thinking it's all his, ignorant as he's always been of everything that goes on outside of the firm and has to do with the flesh-and-blood man at the helm of Araújo, Ltd. But Carlos has turned out to be an ungrateful relation and as the good man I am and always have been, I have the moral obligation never to forgive him. But on the other hand, compelled by the rigorous fulfillment of a duty that in more straitened circumstances would be not only painful but to a degree legally impossible, I have today what to me is the great advantage of a bastard child, so long as one agrees to the condition of loving that child in secret, because such children have the particular advantage of not causing us any unpleasantness that might trouble our dignity, with them we run no risk of seeing our feelings of personal pride trampled on, as we are the only ones to enjoy the sweet wave of pleasure in loving that child, itself a stranger to and unaware of a sentiment it can never deepen. Now, my reasons for complaining of my nephew, which drove me against him, are not only grave but also affect a whole internal family structure put in question by an act of which he is fully aware and that even the least serious person would call unreflective, and that I must call evil. Because my nephew is obliged to admit that if today he is a somebody it's thanks to me, given that I took the trouble to endow him for life with the tools of my hard-earned experience. Because I have always considered schooling the poor man's bread and butter. I know from experience that a high school diploma is enough to steer a youth on to the straight and narrow either here or in Africa where there is no shortage of positions with the local police or of advantageous banking jobs. So just as soon as he came to me I took care to place him in school. Today I recognize that it was a sheer waste of time and money, he has no knack for learning, for five years he did nothing but loaf in class and ended up completing only the seventh grade. And if you add to that the six months he spent in Portugal curing a tuberculosis of the tonsils he brought from S. Nicolau, which had been incubating secretly for years and erupted one day with the violence typical of the disease, obliging me to pack him urgently aboard the *Alfredo da Silva*—you'll begin to get an idea of how much he owes me and how poorly he's repaid me.

It cannot be said that Sr. Napumoceno spoke of Carlos

without a certain tenderness though it is true that he held
against him an offense whose particulars he avoided recount-
ing in his lengthy will, as if concerned with justifying Carlos's
small share of the inheritance, but at the same time wishing to
preserve the offense as a private matter about which it was too
painful to speak. He did, however, write of his decision to put
Carlos to work, seeing that he was clearly averse to books. He
reflected that whether or not he was of any use, Carlos needed
to feed and clothe himself, and so he got him a job as a messenger for the firm Carvalho, Ltd. Perhaps contact with people
who were already adults would awaken in him a sense of
gravity and responsibility for his life and for himself.

Now it is important to note truthfully that notwithstanding
the grave defects that are his, Carlos proved at Carvalho, Ltd.,
to possess qualities that Sr. Napumoceno would never have
suspected in a boy that age and of which he was duly proud,
not only because Carlos was a near relation of his much diminished family, but also because he was the one who had joined
Carlos's name to the firm Carvalho, Ltd. Because from the first
Carlos had shown himself to be unsurpassable at nosing out
business, to have a real knack for acquiring and seducing and
keeping clients, so much so that in the first year he worked as a
cashier he was immediately awarded, by the unanimous decision of the heads of the Business Association and based on
popular consensus, the prize of Cashier of the Year, since it was
a proven fact that no one who passed through the doors of
Carvalho, Ltd., that year and found Carlos behind the counter
left empty-handed, without buying a shirt, a dress, a trinket of
some kind, even if it was only to please that boy who was, in
fact, a real sweetheart, always smiling and joking around. Na-

pumoceno took pleasure in knowing that by his own merit and not thanks to nepotism or to the business relations that had always linked the two firms, Carlos was justly promoted to the level of head cashier right after he was awarded the prize, which afforded him a more comfortable life since he was better paid, and therefore not only an increased sense of well-being but also a certain social prestige. Of course Sr. Napumoceno had always held that there was an ancestral bloodthirstiness in the family that made a degree of aptitude for business natural. He was even convinced that there were Jewish forebears in his genealogy, because, in fact, he still clearly remembered his grandfather selling packets of chewing tobacco, not to mention his own father who earned his daily bread fetching and carrying behind the counter of a village grocery. And though it might be true that he was the only one to get rich from business, it couldn't be said that his ancestors had escaped life in this line of work.

However, seeing the value of this member of the family, he thought it only right to allow Carlos to participate in the success of a firm that in the end was nothing more than the sum of the previous Araújos, especially since it was to the firm that Carlos owed having spent five years lazing around at school and six months strolling around Lisbon, since his tuberculosis of the tonsils never got in the way of his daily walks. So one year at Christmas he invited his nephew for the festive midnight meal with a specially ordered turkey.

Sr. Napumoceno wrote a long and detailed description of that Christmas spent in the house he'd constructed on Alto de Mira-Mar, in which he had had the honor of receiving his beloved and illustrious friends, the excellent Dr. Sousa and his admirable wife. For some time he had been putting off inviting these prized friends to come and get to know his little shack, but in October of that year and on the occasion of a visit to that honored family, Dona Rosa accused him, smiling, of course, of being an ingrate, You can't seem to invite us to see your new house, maybe you're afraid we'd be jealous! So it was that, thus prompted, smiling, albeit modestly and with a certain reserve, he opened his heart, saying that the friendship of Dona Rosa and of the estimable Dr. Sousa was what he valued most in all the world. They were like the dearest members of his family, and he could say without risk of being called a liar that he considered them to be his family in S. Vicente. And so now that the matter had been raised, he would like to request a very special honor: that they agree to spend Christmas Eve in his humble little house in Alto Mira-Mar. He still remembered Dr. Sousa laughing heartily at this long speech which, as he put it, could be summed up as *Come have Christmas dinner with me*, but then he said that they would be very pleased to accept an invitation for a dinner three months off. You probably already have the time set and everything, he added, to which Sr. Napumoceno, smiling humbly, replied that Yes, indeed, it will be at 11:00, though I would also like to have the pleasure of coming to pick you up in my car at 10:00. Sr. Napumoceno did not expect opposition from Dona Rosa, nor was there any. On the contrary, she declared with enthusiasm that at home or elsewhere a family gathering is still a family gathering, it's probably even better, and then gave her consent. So Sr. Napumoceno began right away to busy himself with preparations, it was the first real dinner that he'd given in his life and at his house and on top of that in the friendly presence of such illustrious people, and so he arranged to telegraph to Lisbon for salted cod, turkey, figs, raisins, and other seasonal delicacies, not forgetting the olive oil, because while it may be true that these things are available at the market and the corner store, who can guarantee that this year they wouldn't be sold out?

It was only at the last minute that Sr. Napumoceno decided to invite Carlos to dinner. After all, he was a member of the family, and he was already a fine young fellow, almost a grown man, with the further advantage of having proven himself not to be a fool. And in truth he didn't regret it; he was pleased in fact, that his nephew didn't make him look bad in front of such illustrious guests. Because while he, Napumoceno, and Dr. Sousa were wearing dark three-piece suits, as befitted such an occasion, Carlos showed up in a blue cummerbund and a white shirt and greeted Dr. Sousa with a frank and smiling shake of the hand and a *Nice to meet you, doctor*, and turning next to Dona Rosa he kissed her hand elegantly with an *It's an honor, madame!*, words which very much pleased Sr. Napumoceno and showed him that, school aside, Carlos certainly merited the name Araújo after all.

Certain particulars of the dinner were worthy of the pages of Sr. Napumoceno's will, with ample and special emphasis given to the jokes of Dr. Sousa, who, after the cod and upon seeing the large, golden turkey on the platter, said he needed to loosen his belt because it looked as if what the Araújos intended to stuff was them. And Sr. Napumoceno took the opportunity to repeat a joke of the doctor's in which on Christmas Eve, 1961, two people were jailed after being found in the street, already drunk, shouting Viva Nehru. They were held incommunicado for more than 40 days, wanting to know why they had been jailed, no one knew what to tell them, they were political prisoners, prisoners of PIDE, the secret police, but why they were political prisoners, they were unable to understand, etc., until they were taken to PIDE headquarters, where they were asked what they knew of Nehru, they didn't know who Nehru was, they were asked why then were they shouting Viva Nehru on Christmas Eve, and it wasn't easy for them to explain that they were shouting Viva *peru*—turkey—not Nehru. Sr. Napumoceno also confessed that for him that dinner was an unusually emotional event, especially when the doctor praised his good taste in choosing the wines, and he was unable to stop a tear from falling when it was time for the champagne and Dr. Sousa raised his glass to toast the health and well-being of these youths present here today. I raise this glass with gusto and hope. Silva Araújo proves that this country has its notables, people of value, and that what we need is men like Araújo so that our countrymen may walk with heads held high. I have always thought that a man is the father of himself and Araújo proves I was right. To your health and prosperity.

Deeply moved, Sr. Napumoceno thanked Dr. Sousa for his words, his voice catching in his throat, his glass of genuine French crystal trembling in his hand. He said he was not used to speeches, everyone knew the kind of business he was in, but he couldn't pass up the chance to once again honor the friendship of the doctor and his excellent spouse, Dona Rosa, and he wanted his nephew, who was present here this evening and would one day belong to the ranks of Araújo, Ltd., to know how much he owed to those gathered here today, be it for their friendship and stimulation, or comfort and moral support when encouraging words were what was needed.

As a New Year's gift Carlos received an envelope containing the keys to a metal desk which from that day forward he would occupy at the firm Araújo, Ltd. And for five years he fulfilled his duties with prudence and profit for the company. He seemed to love his work above everything else, while giving the impression of never having anything to do and of always being available for a good laugh. In truth, the work had been greatly streamlined, there was no excessive bureaucracy. Sr. Napumoceno had instituted the buy-sell-profit system, no accounts payable, ledger, or other frivolities beyond what was strictly necessary. And little by little Carlos began to take control of the company, supervising imports himself, selling in his office goods that were still aboard ship, passing on to other merchants the bill of lading for entire shipments of rice, sugar or grain, and showing his reticent uncle that in that way they could sell the goods at a profit while passing on the irritations inherent to Customs, having to do with insufficient documentation and customs declarations and other inconveniences.

Sr. Napumoceno's rigorously honest spirit led him to acknowledge in his will that without a doubt it was Carlos who had propelled and diversified the company's imports toward products that until then had never been seen in the local market, but whose placement proved to be a sure thing. Obviously, Araújo should continue with its rice, its sugar, its cans of lard, but, my dear uncle, the world has changed, the city has other needs and we need to take advantage of this, not sit paddling our boat in little circles. For example, I think it's stupid to continue to insist on exporting orchil and goatskins. There's no doubt that you, uncle, are a personal friend of Ben'Oliel's, but that's true for you, as Sr. Napumoceno. The firm, Araújo, is something else again, and it has its own interests which are often very different from the interests of its shareholders. Look at it this way: What does the company get from exporting orchil and goatskins? A tiny profit that doesn't make up for all the trouble it takes. It makes more sense to focus on imports, to specialize in six or eight brand-name products, well-known and guaranteed, so that whoever buys a case of whisky or gin or a sack of rice from Araújo will always be sure that he's buying products of the highest quality. Because there's nothing like allying the strength of an honored brand to the solidity of the firm.

He also said that, concerned as he was with a variety of other responsibilities, it was not until Carlos drew his attention to it that he noticed how much the city was decaying day by day, the bay almost empty, the ships demanding better-equipped ports. And in these conditions, what market is there left for us? The army, obviously. Because there are more than 1500 men here who have to eat, drink, and smoke. And for a small commission the quartermaster has promised to buy everything from us.

Though happy to see his nephew's commercial vision confirmed, Sr. Napumoceno took pains to cool his youthful ardor. Slow down, boy, slow down. I concede that you're right about some things, but remember age and experience count, and never forget that a man's word is his honor. With this we stand on the strongest foundation, the most sacred ground. I know that youth little esteems these values, but you should never forget them because they are the sturdiest pillars of any organized society. You know, for example, the deal I've made with Ben'Oliel of Boa Vista to receive all the skins and orchil they acquire. Now I can't turn around all of a sudden and say, I'm sorry but from now on I'm only importing, I've given up on exports. And the fact that it's only a verbal agreement takes nothing away from it, on the contrary, to honor it is to honor one's word, a value that grows more imperiled every day.

But he recognized that Carlos was right. In fact, why continue exporting two or three tons of goat skin of inferior quality, or 100 pounds of orchil that the importers said was more dross than anything else, if in truth they gave as much trouble as 100 or 200 tons, and at a profit that wouldn't even buy you cigars? He decided, however, not to proceed in a brutal manner, after all they'd been doing business for many fruitful years, and just because the firm wasn't big didn't mean it didn't deserve the greatest respect. Besides, it was important not to give Carlos too much rope, he'd start thinking every suggestion he made would be religiously observed, and decide to start giving orders right and left. So the firm Araújo, Ltd., Largo da Salina, No. 25, wrote a flattering letter to the Casa Ben'Oliel de Sal-Rei, Boa Vista. Dear Sir: We acknowledge the receipt in our warehouses of two and a half tons of goat skins and one ton of orchil which, we are sorry to report, arrived in lamentable condition due, we presume, to the prolonged journey of the schooner, Sal-Rei, and also to the inadequate way in which they were packed. Unfortunately the quantities, even if the merchandise had arrived in good condition, are insufficient to justify the travails of exportation, especially given that our clients have begun to complain of the inferior quality of the products with which we have supplied them. In fact, for some time now, our firm, purely to maintain a cordial business relationship, has come to sustain a considerable loss in this sector of its trade, which is at the mercy of ever greater demands from its importing clients. Our firm will continue in the future, as it has in the past, to count on preferential treatment from the Ben'Oliel firm in the acquisition of its imported products, but we unfortunately find ourselves obliged to debit those orders with credit extended over 60 days, as a way of minimizing the losses that now befall both parties. Hoping for your most generous understanding, we remain sincerely yours  . . .

Carlos never knew this letter was sent and only many years later did Maria de Graça find it among Sr. Napumoceno's effects. Nevertheless, Carlos noticed that his suggestions were increasingly put into practice, though with small variations that gave them the appearance of being original ideas. Sr. Napumoceno would often call Carlos in to tell him that from one of his suggestions he had conceived during the night an idea that seemed to him to merit attention. Carlos agreed, and he even allowed that his uncle was brilliant, adding that without a doubt night was the ideal counselor. However, in his will, Sr. Napumoceno confessed that he'd laid claim to his nephew's ideas as if they were his own, justifying it by noting that in truth it might well be said that they were, since if Carlos had ideas at all it was because he had sent him to school and then to Lisbon, and that it was even he, Napumoceno, who had gotten him a job at Carvalho's and not somewhere else, so his nephew's ideas were nothing more than the normal return on well-invested capital, and for this reason he considered himself the legitimate owner of any worthwhile notion born in that mind.

But little by little Carlos took the reins of the business and only consulted his uncle out of politeness or in order to divvy up responsibilities. Thus Sr. Napumoceno began to feel he had more time to himself; he was no longer called on to settle every minor matter, and thus was able to dedicate himself to activities he had always loved but that he'd never had time for. And, according to his will, it was at this point in his life that he began to take an interest in world events. For four years he listened to the international news four times a day. And as he had not closely followed the origins and development of World War II, he dedicated himself to ordering from Lisbon just for his own information all that was written on this subject, from simple newspaper accounts to more complex analyses. He said that he left in his library (at an estimated value of 35,500 *escudos*) 23 books on that unhappy slaughter, four books actually written in the theater of war, and a folder with 146 newspaper clippings. He added that because his geography had always been somewhat vague, it was with a globe at hand that he followed the advances and retreats of the troops, though he knew he'd never be able to understand such violence. A child of the islands and for that reason pacific by nature, a man who got goosebumps just from seeing a policeman threatening someone with a billyclub, he would never be able to comprehend such horror. Of course, by nature and social position a humble man, he, Napumoceno, could not aspire to ending the turmoil of the planet. But here on this bit of earth, poor but beloved, he would like to contribute with all his strength to bringing a reign of harmony and peace, and, who knows, maybe even well-being, to the forsaken.

That, incidentally, was the reason he consented to serve on the city council of S. Vicente. Because, contrary to what was said by his detractors, who he knew called him serpent-tongued and gutless, he'd never sought a place at the table or a

crown of laurels, and if it's true that for a while he'd had ambitions of being city council president it was not just for the social prestige of the job, of which he was, naturally, not unaware,
but because of what he felt it would be in his power to do for
his people. In fact, the greatest sorrow of his whole life was
knowing that the same rain that had made his fortune had also
killed dozens of his compatriots abandoned to their fate. And
for that very reason he felt that it was his duty to desire that
position even if the reigning confusion of those times didn't
seem in the least bit propitious, especially because no one
seemed to know any more what was what and who was who in
that bedlam of a political process. In effect, he, Napumoceno,
was witnessing the flight of card-carrying and influential
members of the National Union for the forces of PAIGC, and
was especially confused by seeing the very men who yesterday
had shouted that Portugal was one world from Minho to
Timor, today shouting even louder that independence is the
right of the people, No to a referendum, No to a commonwealth, No to other parties, only PAIGC is the Strength, the
Light, the Leader of Our People. And though he had held as a
lifelong principle that no man has the right to declare himself
neutral, this time he was having a hard time taking a position,
especially given the lack of complete information as to what
was going on. That year, at the very beginning of May, he was
contacted by a delegation of businessmen who had resolved to
intervene politically in Cape Verde and wanted to form a party.
He analyzed the argument they presented to him and admitted
that in fact it might not be completely worthless. They declared that it was necessary to create a force strong enough to
oppose those who were coming in from Guinea, because, it was

said, PAIGC meant communism in our country, disrespect for property, no one would be master of his possessions never mind his wife and children. Didn't he hear it shouted everywhere that everyone has the right to a house and if you have two you'll have to give one of them to whoever doesn't have one? Didn't he see the gangs of kids in the street persecuting people, calling them *catchor dos pé*, running dog, just because they weren't cheering for PAIGC? For all these reasons it was now necessary to show one's opposition to this barbarism both by word and deed and they thought that Sr. Napumoceno should agree to lend his name to this party that would marshal the vital forces of the country, the strength of the city's businessmen, because it was commerce that was the lifeblood of the island.

Sr. Napumoceno wrote that he heard what they were saying and admitted they might be right. They wanted to defend their businesses, which were already threatened, perhaps even with looting, they wanted to defend their property and their families. But at the same time he thought of the others, those who had never had anything, those who might have lunch but don't know if they'll have dinner, those who'd never gone to school because there are no schools, those who fall ill and for whom there is no medicine. He wanted to say that it was those people who died just as easily from rain as from the lack of it who were shouting through the streets in hope, and if they had now discovered a leader to liberate them, he, Napumoceno, didn't feel he had the right to go against them. But he knew he would not be understood and so he decided to say that he felt old and sick, he wanted to concern himself solely with spiritual matters, and the only thing he desired was peace in our land. Hurt, the delegation retreated, and he later heard they accused him of being a traitor to his class. But the truth was that he preferred to shut himself up at home writing the last will and testament of his life, because he no longer recognized himself in all this intolerance so contrary to island ways.

So, while Dona Eduarda told him of the barbarity going on outside, the people who were beaten, how the colonial troops were provoked, the walls painted with pitch, cars set on fire, he took pleasure in evoking the three months he'd spent in Paris, a city he described as open and friendly and filled with affable people; the visit he'd made to Norway to know for a fact what a fjord was; and above all, his 45-day trip to the United States.

Because having seen Carlos moving with ease through the complicated world of business, Sr. Napumoceno finally decided to take a vacation, to enjoy what he had accumulated with effort and tenacity. Up until that day, it had been nothing but work and more work, even of Portugal he knew only Lisbon and one or two other cities in the interior, all visited exclusively on business. So he gave Carlos power of attorney with full authority to manage his affairs and set off, telling everyone he knew what day he was leaving but that his return was in God's hands. And in fact he stayed away for three months, but when he returned Sr. Napumoceno was a different man, wholly unknown to Carlos and to his friends. Where once he'd been calm and slow, he returned nervous, hurried, opinionated, and talkative. For months he talked of nothing but American technology, how moving it was to see a country always concerned with inventing little things to facilitate the lives of people constantly worried about saving time so that they could devote

more of it to work. He even brought back novelties unknown
to the islands, among them a thin plate to be affixed to the
door of his office that connected to a control panel at his desk
which switched on lights of various colors on the plate—green
(come in); yellow (wait); red (busy)—depending on whether he
wanted the visitor or the impertinent fellow to enter or to go
away. Without a doubt technology improves life, it saves effort
and energy, he no longer needed to shout, he had only to turn
on the respective light. But unquestionably his biggest acquisition was a tape recorder that could be hooked up to the phone.
Because this little machine had the intelligence to communicate to whoever called that he, Napumoceno, was absent, and
to ask for and record whatever message the person wished to
leave. But what he considered the height of luxury was a small,
portable device that came with the tape recorder, and that
allowed him, from his house in Alto Mira-Mar, or even from
his car, to activate the tape recorder and listen to the messages
recorded with such fidelity it was as if the caller were speaking
directly into his ear.

Many years later, when there was no longer even the hope
of an inheritance and he could speak frankly of that flaky uncle
of his, Araújo, Carlos told Maria da Graça that it was with an
ironic smile that he'd witnessed the complete change in Sr. Napumoceno's personality and watched him install all those stupid gadgets. In that technological fever he looked like a lunatic
escaped from the asylum, a greenhorn who'd never seen a left-
handed man, while I was killing myself diversifying the imports to guarantee a profit of at least 20% on the docks with
no expenses or problems because if there were any problems they'd be mine to handle, he was already so out of it,

obsessed only with pressing the little buttons, enter, wait, I'm busy, but oblivious to even the kinds of goods we were importing, never mind in what quantity. And, in fact, Sr. Napumoceno would later acknowledge that in truth he allowed himself to be blinded by a technological fever in the first few months following his return from America. And though he was prepared, and duty-bound, never to forgive Carlos the cruel sarcasm with which his nephew had wounded him on that radiant morning and which struck him just as the atomic bomb had struck Hiroshima, he also considered it his duty to declare that in fact he had made too much of the benefits of science and technology, at least as regards our islands, because in the end he'd concluded that the same hand that makes small, marvelous things to delight us makes the most murderous instruments of man's destruction. And following this line of thought, it could as easily be said that we're so poor our docks aren't even equipped with a crane, as that poor we may be but at least we don't run the risk of self-destruction. So, since it seemed to him now that the most important thing was to preserve the placidity of the islands, this backwater of a lost paradise, we must force ourselves to fight tooth and nail against all attempts to place our basic security in danger because what's the use in achieving all the wealth in the world if a man loses his soul? No fortune is enough to make up for the loss of our peace and quiet.

These words Sr. Napumoceno wrote many years after his return from America, when he was a man preoccupied only with spiritual matters, but even so Carlos said it was hard not to burst out laughing when the notary read aloud, in a voice that was so strong it was almost fit for a sermon, the wordy speech of that sly

old dog. Because, according not only to Carlos, but also to the
supplementary documents later found by Maria da Graça, at the
time Sr. Napumoceno was a fierce and rampant defender of
progress at all costs, having even publicly affirmed that—now
this is a good one—if the Americans wanted to install military
bases here—get this—then they should do it, and let them bring
lots of dollars with them. It was Dr. Sousa who threw a little
water on that fire when during one of his visits Napumoceno
raised the issue of the islands' stagnation and spoke of the benefits the American dollar could bring, even pointing to the obvious example of the Azores. In North America he had met some
Azoreans who already felt more American than Portuguese.
However, Dr. Sousa, though listening attentively and without
openly disagreeing, drew his attention to the dangers of a real
war and to the fact that military bases would be prime targets.
Notice that the Americans take pains to establish military bases
outside their own territory because they don't want to run the
risks of war. So we, for our part, should at least leave our people
the peace they have.

These words from a man Sr. Napumoceno considered a
sage cooled his progressive enthusiasms a little, but he continued to think that something ought to be done, and with that in
mind he shut himself in his office and gave himself over to
long, deep meditations, the little red light illuminated in a per-
manent and absolute refusal of entry, I'm extremely busy, I'm
not in for anyone, he would say when they called him on the
inside line. But one day Carlos entered, disregarding the red
light, I'm sorry, uncle, but you know that you cancelled the
power of attorney and we're at risk of losing a shipment of
goods, sign here please. Sr. Napumoceno took little notice of

his nephew's interruption and while he signed Carlos noted that his desk was crammed with biographies of famous men and that the book he was reading was a biography of Abraham Lincoln. What's he up to now, he was thinking when Sr. Napumoceno surprised him with the unexpected question, Did you know that Lincoln was a woodcutter? and with his pen in the air he looked thoughtfully at his nephew. But Carlos, who at that moment could only picture the goods at the bottom of the ship's hold, in danger of making the return voyage, replied that he knew of no such thing, and besides he couldn't have been a real woodcutter because otherwise he wouldn't have made it to such an elevated position, sign the following page, Uncle! Of course there are people who can do anything, he was saying hurriedly, but his uncle, slowly turning the page, added that in fact it was a wondrous and impressive thing that the greatest president of the greatest nation in the world had started out, just like him, Napumoceno Araújo, as a simple woodcutter.

Carlos said that his uncle seemed melancholy that day. He spoke in a thoughtful, almost dreamy way, which was in stark contrast to his serious, wrinkled, and austere face, with only his broad forehead confronting the world, though at the same time he had the look of a startled donkey, with his long ears pointing down.

Meanwhile, smiling, Carlos said, It's too bad we don't have a president in Cape Verde because you, uncle, would get elected. But he confessed to Maria da Graça that at that moment he felt abashed and awkward before that 60-some-year-old merchant who suddenly seemed to be awakening to worlds beyond "have to" and "should," and concerning himself with the lives of other men. But later on Sr. Napumoceno would come to interpret Carlos's smile as mocking, as making fun of his white hair, and he would regret having communicated in a moment of unpardonable weakness his most intimate longings to someone who had demonstrated by his undesirable behavior that he deserved neither the confidence placed in him nor the material blessings whose fruits he enjoyed under the roof of Araújo, Ltd.

In fact, anxious to share with someone he trusted the dream that consumed him of taking on a role in society that wasn't simply about earning money, he had opened himself up at that moment to his nephew. He'd told him that this country was in need of someone who would look out for it and that he, Napumoceno, a member of that great social family by virtue of his wealth, felt capable of dedicating the years that remained to him to the service of the city, the island, and even, who knows, the province. In short, my son, the municipality needs a serious full-time president, and not just a bean counter on the State payroll. It's true, Carlos agreed, impatient, a president of the City Council can do a lot of useful things. But sign here uncle, because the ship won't wait for us and the pork fat may go back.

Sr. Napumoceno had never agreed to relinquish his privilege as the firm's sole and exclusive head, and though usually he signed papers without taking the trouble to read them first, he didn't want to lose this prerogative and feel completely cut off from the company. And in fact, while he was on vacation he had given Carlos power of attorney, with the broadest powers allowed by law, even the special ones of representing him in any government bureau or public establishment, namely the Banco Nacional Ultramarino, depositing and withdrawing sums, receiving summonses and whatever notifications necessary and (just in case, no one knows what tomorrow may bring) accepting inheritances and outright, tax-free gifts—but all this with a set time limit: until his return to S. Vicente. And so, whether it was a letter or a check, he was always the one who signed it, assuming full and complete responsibility for the management of the firm Araújo, Ltd. And, so he wrote, the lamentable facts that forced him to revoke Carlos's status as a member of his family proved he had acted correctly in this particular, by maintaining himself at the head of the firm, if only physically, though it was true that he had never glimpsed the least shade of derision or mockery in the boy until that fateful day.

*S*r. Napumoceno's assertion that he'd been a wood-cutter was considered by Carlos to be nothing more than a figure of speech on the part of a man whose principle defect, as he said to Maria da Graça, was his tendency to exaggerate and make generalizations. Having been raised on S. Nicolau it's totally natural that at one time or another he would have chopped a cord of wood. But to go from that to claiming he'd been a full-time woodcutter at a certain time of his life seems to me to be going a bit too far. But that's the way he was: out of six he always made a dozen.

Graça merely smiled at this bitterness; she wanted to get to know her father at all costs and it seemed to her that Carlos must be the person best qualified to tell her about the deceased. So, always with a smile, she put up with Carlos's occasional gibes at the dead man, reflecting that to have won his friendship at all was already pretty good. But in any case, Carlos only knew the old man's outward traits, since they'd met when he was already a teenager, after he'd lost his father and come from S. Nicolau to live with his uncle in S. Vicente. At

the time, Sr. Napumoceno was still an assistant manager at
João Baptista, Ltd., and it was said that he was constantly pres-
sured by the shareholders to take a small interest in the firm
and become the manager—with a salary four times what he
was earning. But it was also said that he always refused the position, saying he wasn't made for so much responsibility, etc.
Behind his back people whispered that as manager he couldn't
keep cooking the books, as everyone knew he did. And the
truth is that a few years later he left João Baptista and founded
his own business, Araújo, Ltd., Import/Export. Even though
he was the sole owner of the company he added the "limited."
Town gossip had it that this "limit" was the cut he took from
Baptista, and that no one knew if it was large or small. But
right from the beginning, Sr. Napumoceno proved to be, on his
own merits, a businessman of rare intuition or else a man with
incredible luck. It so happened that because his warehouse was
located in Salinas Square he often had to go out there in the
burning August sun, on foot, to top it off, since he didn't yet
own a car and, what's more, didn't even know how to drive. For
that reason he decided to buy a parasol. But it was in vain that
he searched for one in every store and tavern in the city. Not a
single parasol was available for sale and he had to make do
with a cork helmet, with all the inconveniences inherent to the
use of such an accontrement, because being the courteous man
he was he found himself obliged to raise it at every moment in
order to greet those to whom he owed the greatest deference,
thus exposing his forehead to a draft and running the perpetual
risk of a cold, or something worse. And so on one of the several
occasions that he bumped into the traveling salesman and had
to remove his hat to greet him, he complained about this defi-

ciency in the marketplace. And right away the man, laughing loudly, said, If you want I'll get you not one but dozens, hundreds if you like, this shouldn't be the cause of your unhappiness. Well, as it happened, Sr. Napumoceno was already thinking of placing an order with this man and almost as a joke, but conscious that at most it would mean tying up some capital, he placed an order for 1,000 parasols. Best-case scenario he'd sell ten a year, but in any event the market would be supplied, and that would put an end to the disgrace of someone looking all over Mindelo for a parasol and not finding one.

However, when some days later he received the invoice from the traveling salesman he almost had a heart attack. Ten thousand umbrellas in a country where they are used only as parasols since, unfortunately, it doesn't rain. He wouldn't admit that he could possibly have added a zero to the order and so he felt insulted by that salesman who had taken advantage of their friendship in this manner. He sat down right away to write a furious letter. How can you, Dear Sir, continue to count the firm Araújo, Ltd., among your clients after an outrage of this nature . . . but he ripped up the note and went to the post office because only an urgent telegram would calm his rage. Dissatisfied, he wrote, Dear Sir, you fulfilled our contract, tore it up, asked for another form, wrote only, I don't have the words to express my frustration comma, an explanatory letter follows full stop, left, noticed that Sr. Paiva Português was calling him, said *shit* through clenched teeth, but smiled at him and then complained of the wrong that had been done him. Sr. Paiva was a man for whom insoluble problems did not exist, and he advised Sr. Napumoceno to try and place the parasols—or umbrellas, if you prefer—on the islands. Or even in Africa!

Wouldn't it be great if Cape Verde started exporting umbrellas to other provinces? But even that solution didn't suit Sr. Napumoceno, so, taking his leave and trying one last time to console him, Sr. Paiva prophesied that this year it would rain and he'd end up selling all his merchandise. What are you talking about, man! Sr. Napumoceno said, exasperated, This land is cursed! It doesn't rain even as medicine! And he walked away toward the warehouse where he'd left the clerk making a few adjustments, enough to protect the merchandise from the sun until he was able to place it. From the first he had defined himself as a wholesaler: no stores, groceries, counters, or having to put up with people, either employees or the public. He'd gotten more than fed up putting up with the foolery of clients who don't know what they want and dealing with employees who don't know what they're doing. So he'd decided that he and a clerk would more than suffice to run the company. He, Napumoceno, made the contacts, the boy ran errands, hitting the pavement is what young men like. The merchandise came into the warehouse and was sold directly to the retailers depending on the capacity of each but always in boxes, bags, or packages. And while he showed the boy where to put things—he wanted to leave room at the front of the warehouse for a future office—he was mentally drafting another letter to the traveling salesman, a harsh, even offensive letter, so that the man might feel just as humiliated as he, Napumoceno, did. He thought, Dear Sir, scratch that, what Dear Sir, what he really deserves is You son of a bitch, you piece of shit lowlife, you lying scumbag, saddling a small merchant at the start of his career with a cargo of 10,000 umbrellas that won't even be sold off at five a year. "Bad faith" and "rip-off" aren't harsh enough to describe the dishonest way in which you, Dear Sir, cheated me. You, Dear Sir, purposely ignored all the worthy bonds of loyalty underlying exchanges between businessmen, which are the sound principles of good faith and mutual confidence. By sending me a shipment of 10,000 umbrellas, Dear Sir, you cannot ignore the fact that you forced me to invest an enormous amount of capital that I will now be unable to touch until it vanishes altogether, since I don't expect to sell this merchandise at more than five units a year. And I will also state that lacking a reasonable explanation for this excess or any measure that could minimize the losses that you, Dear Sir, have forced me to sustain, our relationship, both commercial and personal, cannot continue except on the basis of absolute mistrust, prejudicial in all events to any sort of common understanding, especially as I will be obliged to communicate to other colleagues that your lack of gravity advises against embarking on even the smallest commercial venture with you, Dear Sir.

The invoice arrived one day, the insulting and threatening letter was sent the next, registered with a return receipt, and the ship with the umbrellas entered the bay on the following day. Fortunately, at that time there were still no air links or regular routes and the mail bag would go whenever it chanced to. As it happened, the ship cast anchor that morning and around midday it began to rain. First it was a fine but persistent rain, a languorous sort of rain as it was called, which led the broadcaster on Radio Club Mindelo to announce that it was drizzling torrentially. But this languorous rain fell all afternoon and night, with overcast skies promising heavier rains, and so the following morning Sr. Napumoceno hurried to clear his merchandise through customs, still in the middle of that drizzle, and as it was already October which is usually a somewhat rainy month, just to assuage his conscience Sr. Napumoceno had it announced on the radio that the firm Araújo, Ltd., had recently received a small allotment of umbrellas and that these self-same umbrellas were at the disposal of local merchants in his warehouses located on Salinas Square. Not surprisingly, the following day he watched 1,000 umbrellas leave the warehouses, covering the cost of 5,000. Meanwhile, only when, three days later, he had already placed 6,000 umbrellas in the marketplace did he reflect that it wasn't worth offending his friend the traveling salesman over such a trifle and he went to the post office, himself armed with an umbrella, and filled out form Model 3 Type C7, asking for the return of his correspondence, and then went back to the warehouse, smiling happily as he passed by Rua de Lisboa, jammed with umbrellas. When he got to the warehouse he found an order for another 2,000.

The rain continued to fall softly and slowly and at rush hour the streets turned into undulating black clouds, everyone laughing happily, the radio station having fun with the rain and the umbrellas: *Protect yourself from the rain with a Better umbrella. The only thing that's better than Better is the rain.* And for eight days the rain fell in that pretty and useful way, soaking the ground, the houses and the streets. And when the last lot of 500 left the warehouse, Sr. Napumoceno ordered champagne for everyone at the Royal, saying he was commemorating the departure of the 10,000.

He acknowledged in his will that it had been a Jew's bargain, made unwittingly and by sheer accident, because sometime later, while going through his papers, he had come across the order, confirming that the mistake of adding an extra zero had been his. Yet, glass raised at the Royal, he boasted of his business acumen, the instinct that had led him to foresee the rain that year, and the great deal he'd just made.

But, as he later lamented, not everything went as he would have wished. Because the rain did not continue to fall as it had in those early days which had been days of plenty of umbrellas and glee and cops in the streets. The very night of the champagne two thunderstorms exploded over the city and the rain poured down cruelly, with unprecedented and brutal force, as if all of a sudden it had tired of coming down softly, and by dawn a fierce gale was blowing. In the morning all you saw were people shivering in the streets of the city, fallen trees, destroyed homes, whole families on the roofs of their houses or on whatever was left of them. Later it was estimated that at least fifty people had disappeared in the floods that passed through the streets of the city, but the furious waters still rushed in in search of the sea, held back only by the walls of the Caizinho.

For the rest of his life, Sr. Napumoceno was unable to convince himself that he hadn't been responsible for that tragedy, and even during his periods of spiritual retreat he was unable to console himself with the idea that one's man's meat is another man's poison, because when he tried to let himself off the hook—he hadn't even knowingly been responsible for the importation of all those umbrellas that might call down heavy rains—his guilty conscience reminded him of the incredible and undreamt-of profit he'd made because he knew that with the sale of 2,000 he'd paid for 10,000. So it was with a heavy heart that he asked to speak with the president of the City Council, and pressed upon him the urgency of doing something for those whom fortune had frowned upon, those whom the blessed rain had left without roof or shelter in the misery of destitution, and volunteered to begin a clothing-and-food drive for the wretched.

This suggestion came as if from heaven. The president of the City Council was utterly disoriented in the midst of all the confusion because, lacking the necessary funds, he'd asked for help from the capital, but the capital was taking its time responding, and the afflicted were still dependent either on the power of whomever was nearest or on whatever came along. The president seized eagerly upon the idea—of course the town's most prominent citizens would have something to say about this tragedy—and gathered the merchants for a meeting (at that time the Business Association did not yet exist).

The circumstances of the election campaign for the presidency led, not Sr. Napumoceno, but his supporters, to make his patriotic act known to the public. However, the profit obtained from the umbrellas was only discovered after the will was read. Sr. Napumoceno had always been a discreet man, despite having been accused of having a tongue as long as his arm. Besides, even this chapter of his life he recounted in order to justify allotting a portion of the yield on his investments to be distributed monthly to decent but needy people. He said that he'd always felt a special tenderness for the shamefaced poor and so he wanted to be remembered once a month by those who waited on his doorstep every Saturday.

He recognized, moreover, that ever since those diabolic rains fighting poverty had become his life's work. Because, after the initial commotion had subsided and the necessary

arrangements had been made, he saw that there was much to
be done. So he started a campaign to repair the destroyed
homes and he himself even traveled to the island of Boa Vista,
not only for some well-deserved rest but to negotiate the pur-
chase of quicklime with the Ben'Oliel firm.

Sr. Napumoceno devoted several piquant pages of his will
and testament to his stay on that island and spoke of what
a privilege it had been to get to know the distinguished Sr.
David Ben'Oliel personally, a man of refinement and the owner
not only of the largest import/export firm on the island but
also of almost all the town dinghies. He spoke of the ecstasy
produced in him by the moonlight on the white sand, and of
the fun had at the dance in Rabil where Sr. David was treated
like a king. But what he still felt a melancholy longing for was
a distant guitar on João Cristão beach the night of a full moon
when the tide was so low that he and his illustrious hosts, Sr.
David and Dona Bibi, could walk on the hard sand of the ebb
tide without getting their feet wet. And, by a happy coincidence, one of Dona Bibi's sisters, usually a resident of North
America, was also spending her vacation on Boa Vista. Living
as they did in the same house—Sr. Napumoceno was after all a
guest of the Ben'Oliels—it was natural that they become
friendly and indeed they took long walks alone on the island's
beaches and spent many hours talking, just the two of them. At
that time, Sr. Napumoceno was somewhere between 45 and 50
and did not deny that he still hoped to marry, have a family, a
wife, a home. Hearing that distant guitar, as they stood with
their feet in that burnished silver sand, the ocean sweetly
crashing near them, he felt that he envied Sr. David who had
been wise enough to flee the confusion of distant lands and

take shelter in this peace of which he was lord and master, with a private family cemetery and his own chapel. But at one point during the walk, when Dona Joia was talking about America, about the constant hustle and bustle, so as a person didn't even have time to scratch her head, a wavelet came near, dangerously threatening her shoes. With peals of silvery laughter and calling the wave a "naughty little wave," Dona Joia, so as not to get her shoes wet, leapt at Sr. Napumoceno, fastening her arms around his neck. Sr. Napumoceno would later confess that, having inhaled that perfume, which though light had a strong effect on his senses, and staggered less by her weight than by her, he felt a word, which happily she did not hear, escape his lips. After all, Dona Joia, already in her forties, but still possessing a youthful freshness, her breasts rich and full as if constantly offering themselves up to caresses, could be considered a very appetizing woman, or to be more up-to-date (in keeping with his sympathetic solidarity with the poor), Dona Joia might be called a real dish. But his regard for his hosts stopped him and it was only at the dance in Rabil, given to bid him farewell, that he dared to tell her, already late into the evening and while dancing a *morna*, that it had been worth getting to know Boa Vista.

However, on the return trip he had more than enough time to reflect because halfway the ship hit a calm and took fourteen days to get to S. Vicente. He ended up concluding that he had been wrong not to declare himself openly to Dona Joia who, through certain words and looks that he patiently and passionately recalled on board, would certainly have been receptive to his offer, not of an immediate courtship, of course, but at least of a warm and friendly correspondence. And he decided that as

soon as he got to S. Vincente he would put a long letter to Dona
Joia in the mail which, not directly yet, but at least between the
lines, would give her to understand his love. He thought of writing her phrases like these: Unfortunately, it is still impossible for
me to reciprocate those agreeable days spent in your company
because destiny, which has protected me in many material ways
(this would serve to make her grasp his solid economic standing), still has not had the goodness to present me with the one
who will be the mother of my children. I believe, however, that I
would not be lying were I to tell you that the days spent in your
company were the happiest of my life, and my only regret is to
have met you in circumstances so constrained that they kept me
from giving free rein to the feelings that enslaved my heart every
time you were near me. I also recall with gratitude our walk
along the seashore on that moonlit night, the distant guitar, and
what happened next. I cannot stop thinking what a pity it is that
faraway America insists on robbing us of excellent wives and
future mothers.

Unhappily, Sr. Napumoceno could not while on board
commit to paper this and other letters that he composed in his
head throughout the journey because his semi-nauseated state
not only did not allow for much movement aboard ship, but
also brought him irrevocably to the brink when he picked up a
book or a pen. For this reason he opted never to abandon his
hammock except to meet obligatory physiological needs and
consigned all his letters to memory, to be transferred to paper
when he got home. But it was impossible to do so right away
because he was faced with a number of pending problems that
first needed to be resolved, having to do with Customs and a
shipment of goods from the firm Araújo, Ltd., which had been

abandoned on the docks—on the grounds that the owner was absent—and then plundered by persons unknown. Sr. Napumoceno did not accept this explanation, contending that for such things were customshouses and the authorities invented, and until it was agreed that he be duly compensated, several anxious days passed during which he had no time to think of love. And as if that were not enough he was then called to City Hall where he was told that the central authorities would look favorably on him were he to present himself as a candidate for city councilman, and not wanting to make excuses he spent a few more days preparing himself to confront the electorate and discussing how he perceived his mission and what could be expected from him. Thus, when he finally had time to sit down and write to Dona Joia, the pretty letters he had thought up at sea were already swept from memory and he could only write that he was running for city councilman and how pleased he would be if she were in S. Vicente to vote for him. The letter, however, was returned; Dona Joia had already left for America.

Given his elected office and the fact that the city had obtained a special fund for reconstructing the houses of those made homeless, Sr. Napumoceno no longer felt the need to occupy himself with this problem specifically, particularly because he already had a voice in the city council and it would in no way do to engage in similar work, as that might be interpreted as a criticism of the typical sluggishness of the public sector. So, he continued to contribute individually to the resolution of these social problems, giving ten percent of the profits on all the quicklime he sold for this construction. As he said, he was not interested in making money from poverty. He wanted profits, of course, but above all on the salt that he sold

to Gambia, the Ivory Coast, and Senegal. Because from his
visit to Boa Vista had resulted a sort of gentleman's agreement
between himself and Sr. Ben'Oliel, according to which he
would buy all the quicklime, salt, orchil, and skins from that
firm, paying for it with whatever merchandise he had in the
warehouse. And, in fact, for years Sr. David's schooners un-
loaded hundreds and hundreds of tons of these articles in
S. Vicente, which Sr. Napumoceno would then ship to more
distant shores.

Finally the moment came when Sr. Napumoceno felt that it
was high time to make the warehouse look like a real firm. So,
in the front, which he had always envisioned as an office, he
built a façade that immediately impressed the whole city with
its importance and sobriety, on which could be read in relief,
painted a dark green on a white background, the words
ARAÚJO, LTD.—IMPORT. EXPORT. The great weakness of Sr.
Napumoceno's life had been Portugal's Sporting Club soccer
team, and by extension any other team that wore the color
green. He thought of green as his tragic flaw, his destiny, and
his luck, and noted in his will that his daughter, Maria da
Graça, owed her existence to the green skirt of Dona Maria
Chica which when he first saw her bent over his desk, he'd
immediately been seized with the urge to lift . . . But that
part of his life is still a long way off, right now he is preoccupied only with the firm's façade: on the outside, an office build-
ing; inside, an open warehouse covered in French roofing tiles.
In the meantime he had two offices built, a more elegant one
for himself, another for an assistant, and in the back he had
an enormous gate installed on metal runners so as not to
waste space, and divided the area meant for merchandise

into several sections with signs for sugar, rice, butter, lard, and so on.

But the truth of the matter was that the warehouse was almost always empty of merchandise due to the fact that Araújo, Ltd.'s, first import had been a shipment of rice. It so happened that not a single grain of rice had been available in the market and once it was known that Sr. Napumoceno was awaiting rice the retailers had invaded his office, and even refused to leave him alone in his own house. So before the rice could even enter Cape Verdean waters, it was all already sold, and then went straight to the stores. This was the incident that made Sr. Napumoceno realize he could actually sell on the docks, since he saw that he had everything to gain from importing and selling the merchandise just as it left its point of origin. Nonetheless, he concerned himself with furnishing his office and a short time later he built two rooms in addition to those that were already there, and moved his office into them. And since it had already been decided that he would hire a secretary, he constructed a carpeted reception area with Naugahyde sofas, as was the fashion, magazines and newspapers displayed on a table in the center of the room, and near the door of this office, a desk that in future would be his assistant's. Only after returning from America did it occur to him to install an electronic lock, the kind that can be opened by pressing a button.

He wanted his office to be a place of business but also a retreat and so he took care to furnish it with some regard to its function, but above all with taste and sobriety, as suits a man lacking in ephemeral vanities and more interested in eternal values. He earmarked the right wall for a shelf to hold folders and books related to business, leaving the left wall for a shelf to

house his recreational reading. On the wall that remained in
front he placed only a reproduction of the Mona Lisa. But the
centerpiece of Sr. Napumoceno's office, which unquestionably
dominated the room, was his desk. It was a massive piece of
furniture, with legs sculpted into lions that held up the wood-
and-glass top, and Sr. Napumoceno liked to say that it was the
only example of Louis XV furniture in S. Vicente, maybe even
in all of Cape Verde. He had bought it when it was practically
in pieces and had asked Sr. Rafael to proceed with its repair, so
it would look like it had just come from the factory. And in
truth Sr. Rafael took great pains in his refurbishments and so
perfectly did the work turn out that he couldn't resist saying to
Sr. Napumoceno, thereby securing his undying enmity, that
such a work of art would sit better in the office of a thinker
than in the hands of a wholesaler. What is certain is that
the desk turned out to be of great use to Sr. Napumoceno and
Dona Chica, because, strong and resistant, it supported them
without a moan as he mounted her, whether Sr. Napumoceno
was standing in front of the green skirt, cocked and ready and
firing with legs spread wide, or Dona Chica was on all fours,
Sr. Napumoceno moving with care from behind.

Obviously, Sr. Napumoceno was not the kind of man to
speak with such bravado in his will, having limited himself in
this regard to saying that Maria da Graça was conceived hugging the desk, the mother always in the green skirt. And if
Graça hadn't taken such care to find out what there was to
know about her origins, these particulars would have remained
forever obscure. She had grown up calling Nho Silvério *father*,
and had had only a vague idea that there was a pension that allowed her to attend high school. She knew that Nho Silvério

wasn't her father, but by the time she reached the age when she could begin to discuss such details with her mother she knew enough about unwanted children to prefer to think of herself as having been the fruit of a slip-up. And when, returning from work on the day Sr. Napumoceno died, she'd found her mother on the canvas chair being nourished with glasses of sugar water, she took fright, hugging her, and her first thought was of heart trouble, but it never crossed her mind that the news of Sr. Napumoceno's death was what had put her into that state, even though she knew her mother was a pensioner of Araújo, Ltd. Moreover, her mother took care to reassure her, I'm better, but it was a great shock for us.

What happened to you, mother? Graça asked. What was a big shock for us?

*Chenchene!* Dona Chica said. *Our pension.*

It never occurred to Graça that Sr. Araújo might be Chenchene. She was, in fact acquainted with Sr. Napumoceno, he had spoken with her a few times already, taking a great interest in the progress of her studies while she was a student, but always at chance meetings; they would happen to meet, usually at the end of each term, and he would happen to have chocolates in the car to offer her. But it was always Sr. Araújo, no Napumoceno, much less Chenchene, a name that she was hearing now for the first time. So, when her mother spoke of Chenchene and a pension, what Graça realized, alarmed, was that her mother was getting a little soft in the head. Who is Chenchene, she asked, but her mother had already come to her senses, she preferred to silence herself with a coughing fit, and then, thanking the neighbors for their help, she asked Graçinha to help her get up, and went into the house. And

once inside she explained to her daughter that Chenchene, Sr.
Napumoceno Araújo who had just died, was a great friend of
hers and it was he who had given them the pension on which
they lived. Without it she would have been at God's mercy.
Graça laughed at those tragic words. Did you also lose your
daughter? she asked. And it was only after the last will and testament had been read that she learned, at the same time as
everyone else, that she was the daughter of the deceased, heir
to the name and to the fortune. She was surprised at home by
the unexpected arrival of one Sr. Fonseca, Américo Fonseca,
my dear, at your service! But it was a sweaty Sr. Fonseca covered in dust and with dirt on his shoes, who had run all over
Ribeira Bote, Bela Vista, and Lombo do Tanque in search of
the house of Dona Maria Francisca, mother of Miss Maria da
Graça, but with all those names no one knew who she was,
Dona Maria Francisca was just Nha Chica, wife of Nho Silvério, Miss Maria da Graça was Graça or Graçinha, daughter
of Nha Chica, so no one could say who they might be, I don't
know them, I don't know, maybe back there somewhere, etc.,
until someone suggested that it was probably Nha Chica,
mother of Graçinha, he was looking for. And in fact it was. Sr.
Fonseca asked permission to enter, he said he needed to speak
with the mother and the daughter, he was bringing important
news of interest to them both. Graçinha was in the backyard
washing her feet—they lived in a house without a bathroom,
forget running water, for light only a kerosene lamp and thanks
be to God for that—when Sr. Fonseca coughed, Graçinha entered wiping her feet, and seeing that man in a suit, said, Good
evening. Sr. Fonseca got up from the chair that Dona Chica
had offered him, and taking Graçinha's hand, he kissed it and

with a low bow said, Congratulations. Faced with Graça's surprise, he explained that for more than two hours he'd been
searching for their house. On no account did he want to leave
these good tidings for the next day. He had begun his search in
the company of Lima, but Lima had finally given up, after
much walking, and returned home because his shoes were
hurting his feet. But he had persisted, he was known as a stubborn man, and now he was rewarded. He smiled and said that,
according to the wishes of the deceased, may God keep him,
he was one of the witnesses to the solemn reading of the last
will and testament of his beloved and dearly missed friend Napumoceno da Silva Araújo and was here to bring the very
pleasant news that from that day forth Miss Maria da Graça
would be able to add to her pretty name the surname Araújo,
honored above all others in this city. And he also added that by
the express will of the dearly departed, in accordance with the
testamentary clause, she was hereby established as the sole heir
of all his property, obliged only to satisfy certain charitable
legacies.

   At first Maria da Graça did not understand the good tidings, at first she just thought that it was kind of funny, the way
Sr. Fonseca talked, with a lot of gestures, his mouth twisting, as
a fine mustache danced above it, and when Sr. Fonseca got up
and said, My belated but still deeply felt condolences!, she
thought he was getting up to say good-bye and said, Thank
you, until next time!, and Sr. Fonseca somewhat flustered but
promising to return the following day to explain things further,
departed, leaving mother and daughter alone, the next-door
neighbors right outside the house.

   Until then, Gracinha had been a sweet and affectionate

daughter, but on that day she lost it, demanded explanations, at
first shouting because she didn't understand anything, then
sobbing, kneeling on the cement floor with her head in her
mother's lap. She later told Carlos that she'd never felt the absence of a real father because Sr. Silverio loved her a lot and
so she had never thought that a real father was a necessary part
of a child's life, especially since one thing there's plenty of in
this country is fatherless children. So she'd never asked her
mother any questions, not only to spare her from remembering
things that might be sad for her to recall, but also because she
didn't miss having a father. And when she saw so many
fathers nagging their kids she would even thank God that
there was no one to nag her. But at that moment she felt that
she had lost a father whom she had never even known, though
at the same time she was angry at herself for lamenting this
fact. But, on the other hand, she began to feel upset thinking of
that old man who had looked at her with great tenderness in
his eyes, as if he wanted to devour her, and she could once
again picture the old man asking her about her grades, grasp-
ing of her hands in his aged trembling ones, Take special care
with geography, that was always my weak point! And his
opportune way of having chocolates in the car when he said
good-bye, God bless you!, and she would remain standing
there looking at the crazy old man, and so on that night, after
her mother had told her how it had happened, she'd cried,
lying down in her room, not from longing but from pity and
remorse for the suffering stamped on that wrinkled face which
looked at her with the eyes of a kicked dog, and when she finally fell asleep it was to dream that she was kissing her father
and was giving him all the affection he'd asked for with those

eyes starved for tenderness, even though her mother had told her the truth of the matter and that truth was neither as beautiful nor as poetic as she had always dreamed it should be—it had not been a question of an impossible love except for the fact that her mother was only a cleaning woman. When Sr. Napumoceno had asked her to clean his office, Dona Chica had accepted because she needed a regular job and this seemed like a good one, with short hours, she just had to get the work done and then she could go home. She arrived at around 7:00 in the morning, cleaned the adjacent rooms, and every day at 8:00 Napumoceno opened up the office and immediately went out to go about his business, barely a word was exchanged because he wasn't a man much given to conversation, often they didn't say much more than Good morning, Sr. Araújo! Good morning, Chica! At first she'd called him Sr. Napumoceno but he hadn't liked it saying that only servants were called by their first names, so she'd begun to call him only Sr. Araújo, for me it was the same, one name or another, often after that *good morning* she didn't even see him again, until one day, she remembered it perfectly, as if it were yesterday, she also remembered that it had been a Saturday because on the following day there had been an important game between Sporting and the Mindelense to determine who would win the championship and it even happened that on the following Monday Sr. Araújo found her at the door to his office and told her with a smile that she had brought them luck because Sporting had won the day before, 3-0, and, smiling now as she recalled that day, she said that she neither smiled at him nor congratulated him, on the contrary she continued to make a long face, she was still mad about his behavior on the previous Saturday, because on that

Saturday, she remembers having gone to work wearing a green taffeta skirt and a white blouse and she was just cleaning the desk when he came back in, but he stopped in the doorway looking at her, as if he had never seen her before, with his eyes open wide—at that time he was still not completely bald, on the contrary you could even say he was an attractive man—and he stood stock-still staring at her, and she looked back, interrupted her cleaning, laughed shyly, said, What's wrong with you sir, you look like you've seen a ghost, but he didn't respond or smile, simply continued staring, his Adam's apple rising and falling as if he'd swallowed couscous without chewing it first, she said again, my goodness man, you scare a person, sir, but he remained silent at the door, only his Adam's apple going up and down, but suddenly he closed the door, turning the lock; she, Maria Chica, didn't understand at first, who would have imagined something like that from a man of his social position and so respected, but he approached her and said something like Excuse me and grabbed her and bent her double over the desk, she fought, said, Let go of me or I'll scream!, and at the same time felt him straining to lift her skirts which she managed to clasp between her legs, but bent double over that mahogany desk that was so strong and heavy it didn't even groan or move, she felt her back start to hurt so she adjusted herself to be more comfortable and he took advantage and was able to open her legs and lift her skirts while she punched his head, and, smiling again, she said that he didn't even seem to feel her blows, so beside himself was he, and he pushed her panties aside and she could only think to say, You're going to rip them!, but it seemed like he didn't even hear her, he was deaf and blind, and in one motion he buried himself in her and emptied

that hot substance in her and remained lying on her gasping
for breath as if he were having the hiccups, and she lay still,
worried that the man had entered his death throes, but little by
little he composed himself and she no longer knew whether
she ought to get mad or to go away, he was still on top of her,
but she could feel the beginnings of pins and needles in her
legs and told him so, and he only said, Forgive me in the name
of whomever you love most!, and she heard the anguish in his
words, felt the pain of that man wallowing in his own shame,
understood the weak gesture with which he moved away from
her, buttoning his fly, and then she felt immense pity for him,
and looked at him, and said, May God always give you wisdom!, and began to clean again as if nothing had happened and
Sr. Napumoceno opened the door and went out and she saw
him in the street walking as if he were drunk first thing in the
morning and thought *Poor man! Men are so pathetic!,* and so she
finished her work and went home and returned that happy
Monday when Sporting were already champions. But that day
Sr. Napumoceno was cheerful and playful and talked with her
about her work, about whether she earned enough, whether
she'd gone to the game, but it was as if that Saturday between
them had never happened because in more than half an hour of
conversation there was not one reference to it. Only when she
was getting ready to leave did Sr. Napumoceno get out his wallet and reach in to give her 500 *escudos* to celebrate Sporting's
victory.

Graça said this was the only moment when she wanted to
interrupt her mother, to ask if she had accepted the money, but
she couldn't make a sound and simply lifted her head and
looked at her with wide, pleading eyes waiting for her to finish,

but during that part her mother paused for some time and so she again buried her face in her lap and continued sobbing with shame until she heard her say, No, no thank you, I'm not a whore to lay down with a man for money.

Sr. Napumoceno remained silent for a long while, as if embarrassed, but then he picked up the money and his wallet, and said simply, I've offended you a second time, I beg your pardon once again. And he left and days went by with Sr. Napumoceno's strangled *good mornings* and with no other exchange of words, but when Dona Chica again came to work wearing the green skirt and white shirt he again locked the door. Only on that day he was not embarrassed, on the contrary he was playful and in a good mood, and he paused on purpose along the way, explored, moved around, went in and out, and only when she started to moan did he begin a furious gallop, and she bit her lip in order not to scream and he said, What a woman!, and on the occasions that followed there was no need for the entrapment charade, Why, if we both wanted it, only it was always on top of the wooden desk which I hope is still there because as a bed it was hard but as a desk it was perfection.

*E*veryone had something to say when Sr. Napumoceno left João Baptista, Ltd., and his detractors were particularly shameless in claiming that it was because he'd already had his fill that now he was loosening his grip, he must be stuffed to the gills with money, they've probably already turned off the tap so now he wants to steal on his own account, together with, of course, more flattering opinions such as, A thief who steals from a thief is pardoned for a hundred years; he was a thousand times right to have stolen from Baptista who's done nothing but rob this city, just look at the poor people who watched as their houses were mortgaged and sold at auction to repay Baptista's loans with their never-ending interest. There was even talk of the well-to-do property owner from Santo Antão whom Baptista drove to suicide over a debt of 30 *contos* that in two years had reached 200 *contos* because of the interest he charged and compounded monthly. The firm João Baptista was rumored to own half the houses in S. Vicente and it was said that it was only because they had no interest in the other half that they left the rest on the market.

At that time the court was overloaded and had to move quickly, whoever bid more won, so João Baptista was hated and feared and anyone who stole from him deserved to be praised. However, no one was ever sure, because he never told anyone nor wrote it down anywhere, how much capital Sr. Napumoceno possessed when he left his job as assistant manager at Baptista, Ltd., and the only thing anyone knew for sure was that he was already the owner of that "soccer field" in Salinas, acquired at an auction set up by João Baptista for the value of the debt, even though it was worth almost ten times as much.

At that time Sr. Napumoceno was a cheerful young man and he remained cheerful as he bid in the third auction; the first auction was for the real value of the warehouse and no one wanted it, it was said that everything had already been arranged among those who had money; the second auction was for the value of the debt plus half, and again no one wanted it; and the third time, he showed up alone, and ended up lord and master of that world.

The former owner publicly accused Sr. Napumoceno of being a small-time cheat from S. Nicolau who had come to rip off decent folk and for two days he wandered the offices of João Baptista calling them highway robbers, exploiters of the people, The day will come when someone will catch you, you pack of greedy thieves. He shouted so that everyone would hear and it was Pé de Pulguinha who calmed him down, Don't worry, Diogo, Sr. Baptista will agree to adjust the mortgage, so that later, when it was too late, when Diogo could no longer do anything about it, Pé de Pulguinha could come in the name of that bastard Baptista invoking the Bank's needs, the mortgage was already foreclosed, it was just a matter of execution, seizure, a public sale by court order. But when his tirade went on for a third day, the police came straightaway, You're under arrest for disturbing the peace, summary trial. Dioguinho was given a suspended sentence on the condition that for five years the names João Baptista and Napumoceno Araújo would not pass his lips. But years later, when Sr. Napumoceno was a well-regarded businessman, with a reputation in the trade and the social standing that his personal fortune afforded him, he hired Dioguinho as a night watchman for the firm Araújo, Ltd., since, after all, whoever doesn't know how to forgive a wrong doesn't deserve to be called one of God's children.

But even if no one would ever know for sure how much he'd made off with from João Baptista, it was said that doubtless both had benefited for he no longer had a boss and Baptista had one less thief. Nonetheless, during the electoral campaign for City Council, when people heard of the work he had done in collaboration with the city council president at the time of the tragic floods, and of the lengths he had gone to, and even of the trip he had made to Boa Vista with the sole goal of obtaining quicklime with which to reconstruct the houses of the poor that had been destroyed by the floods, the halo of a man keenly attuned to the problems of the poor began to surround Sr. Napumoceno. It goes without saying that he denied this deed, he was just a poor businessman who helped out when he could, thanks were owed, yes and many, to the president of the city council, he was simply a businessman who offered advice based on his own experience and familiarity with poverty, and of course the idea of quicklime had seemed like a good one to him because it was cheaper . . .

But the truth is, it began to be noted that Sr. Napumoceno
sent for quicklime from Boa Vista at his own expense and
donated it to the City Council for construction projects for
the poor. When he was questioned directly, he neither confirmed nor denied this, but limited himself to smiling and saying that, Yes, in fact, he had been in Boa Vista, he'd made the
acquaintance of the great businessman of the island, Sr. David
Ben'Oliel, and of course they'd talked about the disaster that
had hit the poor of S. Vicente and so it was natural that being
the great man he was Sr. Ben'Oliel would place his services at
the disposal of the people, as indeed would anyone with the
means of doing so. He, Araújo, was just another element, the
necessary catalyst perhaps, to get things to happen quickly. But
in this regard he acted out of duty to his city, as a man who
came from nothing and now enjoyed greater comfort than
most. He had not been thinking of business, because from a
business perspective this would yield nothing but trouble.

What is certain is that Sr. Napumoceno began to export
salt, goat skins, and orchil. Salt to Africa, the rest to Europe,
and in exchange received articles he was sure to be able to place
on the national market, articles that were either sold on the
docks or transferred straightaway to the little boats that served
the islands. So though it was thought to be a hefty sum, no one
really had a concrete idea of what his fortune amounted to, not
even Carlos ever knew the extent of his uncle's means and
holdings, even though the reins of the business were in his
hands. Because, as if intuitively, Sr. Napumoceno always put
off giving him a full account, You're still too young to understand certain things, with time and little by little you'll come to
understand everything. For his part, Carlos knew only that

there were a lot of things he wasn't privy to, things his uncle didn't allow to pass through his hands. In time, the only thing Carlos came to understand was that his uncle was a pensive, introverted man. Once, before the automated lock, when he walked into his office without asking permission he found him seated at his desk, completely still as if he had died sitting down, with his eyes open and Carlos would have screamed with fright if Sr. Napumoceno hadn't spoken to say *A closed door is like the continuation of a wall, it should never be opened without permission.* Carlos told Maria da Graça that without a doubt there were two Napumocenos: the one before America and the one after. But I think I liked the other one better, the one before America. Because when he returned, he even brought a new car with him, saying that in America a car has a shelf life of two years and to keep it longer was to throw money away. But he didn't have the courage to sell the green Ford, he let it rot in the garage. Besides, he never got rid of anything. His theory was *keep what you can't use, you'll find what you need.* In the end, he never stopped being a poor boy from S. Nicolau.

And in fact the old Ford was found in the garage, eaten by rot and with a rusted engine, and though the will asserted that it was worth at least 120 *contos*, it was obvious that it wouldn't pay even to throw it away. Careless old man, Sr. Fonseca said, letting off steam. Allowing a veritable museum piece to go to waste, one that in normal circumstances would be worth a fortune. It was a dark-green Ford, a Model T from 1918, that Sr. Napumoceno had ordered the year after those fateful rains. He'd decided to be the first person to drive a car on this island and only when it had already gone through customs did he re-

member that he neither had a license nor did he know how to
drive. But still he refused to allow anyone else to be the first to
show off his vehicle and the whole town turned out when he
crossed the Rua de Lisboa at the wheel of his Ford, pushed by
four men.

With the car locked in the warehouse that served as a
garage, he applied himself to learning to drive under the tute-
lage of Nho Isidoro, an experienced but rigorous instructor
with some less-than-pleasant words on the tip of his tongue
for punishing the inept. When it was just a matter of following
the road straight ahead everything went well and there was no
reason for complaint on either side. It was in maneuvering the
car that difficulties began to arise, because Sr. Napumoceno
couldn't master putting it into reverse, and one day when he
turned the car too far, Nho Isidoro, who was in the middle of
the street and was directing him from a distance, shouted at
him to straighten that piece of shit. But at that point Sr. Napumoceno put his foot on the brake with such violence that the
car stalled. Not realizing what was happening, Nho Isidoro
kept screaming, Not there, for the love of God!, but Sr. Napumoceno was already out of the car, his face expressionless,
I'm the one who decides how my money is spent and I won't
stand for insolence or bad language from anyone. I know that
you have a famously filthy mouth, but either you apologize immediately or I'll revoke the contract right here and now and go
home on foot. They were somewhere near Ribeira Julião, but
even so Nho Isidoro saw he was in for it and he tried to convince Sr. Napumoceno that he'd had no intention of giving offense, it was simply a figure of speech, but only after a formal *I
ask you to pardon my vulgar language!* did Sr. Napumoceno agree

to get in the car again. Thus he never did learn to back up, a maneuver that he declared extremely dangerous, so dangerous that the Traffic Code itself forbids it for a distance of more than five meters! And so the garage at his house was a large corridor with an exit on either end and he never parked anywhere where he would be obliged to commit that infraction of the code. But the rest he learned easily enough because he took advantage of the warehouse to practice in the Ford for two hours every day and so on the day he got his license and went out in the car no one dared to say, Look, there's a man who has just passed his driver's test. What everyone said right away—and even in the years that followed—was that it was doubtless the cleanest and best-kept car in the city and it's true that Sr. Napumoceno hired someone just to clean the car, and that person, shut up in the warehouse from 9:00 until noon every day, cleaned, scrubbed, and polished the car and always kept flannel cloths in the glove compartment to wipe wherever some daring or careless person had touched the car with his hands. In his will, Sr. Napumoceno said that it was with true and unfettered pride that he could attest to never having had a single accident no matter how minor, nor a single ticket for breaking the law, nor the least censure from the relevant authorities in almost 40 years of driving.

It seems, however, that after he got his license Sr. Napumoceno decided to start a family. Not that he made explicit reference to this decision in his will, and no one would ever have known about it if Graça, in her zeal to get to know her deceased father, hadn't forced herself to decipher the scribbled pages he'd left all over the house, which offered a wealth of material on a woman named Adélia, who seemed to have left a

decisive mark on the life of the dead man. In his will he did
speak in detail of his nascent love in Boa Vista, but said that
the attempt having failed it was many years before he thought
for the third time of starting a family, of setting up house like
any decent man. Having, in fact, confided this noble desire to
someone whom he considered part of his closest family, that
person, perhaps motivated by petty interests, advised against
such an initiative, making explicit reference to his age. And he
had ended up resigning himself to the situation in which he
would finally end up dying. Because of this passage, Maria da
Graça badgered Carlos, saying simply, He can only mean you,
my dear cousin, because I wasn't yet part of the family. But
Carlos defended himself, he didn't remember anything of the
sort, the guy was too full of himself ever to accept my opinion
on something like that, he was the sort of person to get married and only tell me the next day, I'm convinced he's putting
on another one of his acts. But then he remembered that, in
fact, one day when he'd found his uncle brooding and had ex-
pressed concern about his sadness and had asked him if things
weren't going well, the old man had replied that, No, as far as
business went everything was running very well in fact, but he
felt very alone, very alone in that big house and so he was
thinking of getting married. Carlos said that he'd said, Yes sir,
good idea, uncle, you do need a companion, you've worked for
it. And I don't doubt that you, uncle, will know how to pick a
bride from among the women of your social circle, because
given your age and your position just anyone won't do. You're
over 60, aren't you? Sr. Napumoceno said that he was already
65 and that he still didn't have a fiancée. Just thoughts. That's
what happened, nothing else, Carlos concluded. If he didn't get

married it's because he didn't want to and now the ingrate blames me.

Thus, having discovered nothing concrete about her father's third attempt at matrimony, Graça devoted herself to finding the Adélia in Sr. Napumoceno's life and ended up with a pretty precise idea both of the love affair itself and of its unhappy unraveling because, though omitted from the will, Adélia was the subject of five 24-page school notebooks, and still other sundry writings devoted entirely to her. In the first notebook, Sr. Napumoceno declared that he had decided to make known to posterity, as an example to and for the edification of whoever might read it, the tragic love affair that more than anything else in the world had upset his life. But he began by saying that he knew that he was said to have made his fortune in contraband liquor and gems, assertions that he neither confirmed nor denied. However, only a fool could think that such an accusation would embarrass him because it had never entered his head that contraband was a sin. On the contrary, he felt that the levying of more customs taxes was only a form of extortion, the State sticking its hand in everyone's pockets and offering nothing worthwhile in return. Thus, personally, he preferred to split that fiscal fraction with others and in less demanding portions than the State's. However, once he'd set up for himself he'd abandoned these defiant ideas as he'd also given up on a certain kind of socializing in the taverns of Lombo, in the company of women of doubtful virtue. Not that he was any less of a man. On the contrary, on many a night given over to clandestine activities he'd proved, though discreetly and with no boasting, to be man enough for any woman, even the most demanding. But what had really prompted him to change his life was that as he was making his rounds of local dives he'd met a woman from Dakar, a woman to make your mouth water, who'd been around the block certainly but wasn't a prostitute and who'd turned every man's head with her promises of dreamy bedroom delights, promises that no one had yet made flesh. Sr. Napumoceno met her and decided that he had to sleep with her. He embarked on such a gallant and persistent courting, with dinners and walks and presents and parties, that by the end of a week he had triumphed where all the others had failed in more than a month's time. It was only one night, but Sr. Napumoceno would remember it his whole life as a glorious night because the woman from Dakar pleasured him with gestures and words and caresses that were absolutely unknown to him and when she proposed what he would from then on always call *voulez-vous descendre la cave*, he descended and dove and lost himself and took pleasure in the cave for a whole night. But the next day she'd already vanished into the city and for three days he searched for her like a madman in every dance hall and bar in Mindelo without finding her and he persisted in his search because he felt that at the very least that night merited a sequel. She'd initiated him into caresses he'd known only from books and even then hadn't understood very well, and for that reason he refused to lose her without saying good-bye. But on the third day he began to feel a burning whenever he peed and on the fourth he knew for sure that she'd given him the clap. Dreamy night or no dreamy night, he decided to give her a beating that would make her ache all over, and he searched for her even more zealously through the streets and taverns of the city and in every place he thought might be a flophouse or a tavern, until he discovered that she'd left town again. Embarrassed, he allowed two weeks to go by without seeking treatment and had to submit to huge doses of "914" for a cure of whose efficacy he could be convinced only after lengthy exams with a competent specialist in Lisbon, since his greatest concern was to find out if it was possible to get that thing in his mouth, but he couldn't bring himself to the point of actually admitting that he'd been sloshing his mustache in that slime. So from then on he adopted the habit of always carrying toothpaste in his jacket pocket for fear of being surprised by some less-than-agreeable odor.

But after he turned 50 and was already firmly established in the marketplace, a respected councilman who was definitively cured of his trouble, and ready for another, as the doctor in Lisbon had said, Sr. Napumoceno thought it high time to start a family, especially now that his fear of the diseases of the world kept him at home. However, and this is a fact, it must be said that he'd never done more whoring or more screwing around than other men—or at least no more immoderately than anyone else. He'd always been a methodical person and even in his youth he'd prided himself on benefiting from salutary influences. And during the years Carlos spent with him he drew his attention almost daily to the necessity of considering the opinions of his elders. Someone who doesn't know how to listen, who doesn't have the most basic principles of respect for his elders, cannot aspire to be esteemed as an adult. A well-brought up young man embraces obedience as his principle tenet—so Sr. Napumoceno taught, and in truth he couldn't be accused of contempt for useful advice. He'd come from S. Nicolau as a barefoot boy, landing at the customs dock with a huge, almost empty suitcase since he had only two pairs of

pants and three shirts and a few pennies in his pocket. An old
aunt who lived in Fonte Filipe was his only contact on the island and when a porter named Jovita said to him, I'll take your
suitcase, and he said, Fonte Filipe, home of Nha Guida, and
she, already making a cloth pad for her head on which to place
the suitcase, said, It's very far, he became frightened because he
had no idea what she was going to charge, he only knew that
here things were very different than in S. Nicolau where he
could have carried his own suitcase. He crossed the Rua de
Lisboa, the Largo do Palácio, and climbed the Fonte de
Cónego, trotting after Jovita and delighting in the marvel that
was Mindelo. He'd never seen so many people at once and felt
embarrassed at being barefoot as he followed the woman
porter in her plastic sandals. That day he didn't leave home,
afraid of getting lost in the enormous city or of being attacked
by bandits—he knew they existed and preyed on people night
and day. And even when he was told by his aunt to calm down,
it wasn't quite that bad, something might happen but it hadn't
gotten to the point where people were robbed in broad daylight, he walked around at first with the pocket in which he
kept what little money he had fastened with a safety pin. But
two days later, by the time his aunt said he needed to buy plastic sandals, he'd already realized that he needed to stick those
untamed feet into shoes. And so he bought sandals for every-
day wear and sneakers for Sundays.

Sr. Napumoceno had brought with him a package, a pipe
made from rubberbush wood that an uncle of his had sent for a
Dr. Gilberto Sousa, who was a big shot in S. Vicente, but an
old friend from school. After he arrived, two weeks passed before he gathered the courage to present himself and deliver the

gift, but he was surprised when the doctor, after asking about his uncle and life in S. Nicolau, said that the first thing he had to do was try to get some sort of job and offered to help him in any way he could.

Near the end of his life he would say that he owed his first job to a rubberbush pipe in the shape of a goat's head. Because thanks to Dr. Sousa, a few days later he started at Millers as an errand boy, in a city he didn't know, and for that very reason he got to know it quickly and well. Quite soon he felt as at home as he did in S. Nicolau, with acquaintances on every corner, and it didn't take long before he began to be invited to Saturday night dances and even to parties in private homes. But he made a point of visiting the doctor every Sunday afternoon because he felt so pleased and honored that a man with an advanced degree would listen so attentively to him as he recalled life on his native island. One day he spoke of the bad reputation S. Vicente had in S. Nicolau; it was said to be a land of perdition, a kind of Sodom and Gomorrah, once you came, you never escaped . . . But the doctor just smiled, S. Vicente is the same as any other place, the thing is to know how to make friends, and to be careful of the company you keep. Because here you have opportunities you'd never have in S. Nicolau. There it's grade school and then the plow. But here if, for example, you want to study at night, you can have private tutoring and take your exam at the end of the year. Obviously, you might prefer to go to the movies and to bars instead of studying. But the truth is that here you have more opportunities than you do on any of the other islands.

Sr. Napumoceno could never say whether he'd taken up his studies because of an innate bookishness, or Dr. Sousa's influence, or a bet he'd made with a friend. Because the following year he began to attend middle school with a friend from work, who said he wanted to get on the straight and narrow but who always dropped out mid-year, and three years later he completed high school. He felt proud of his work and of having learned like Dr. Sousa that the first thing that makes a man is self-respect and that only after very serious consideration should an adult stop doing something he thought was worth doing in the first place. He prided himself on having risen in life by pulling himself up by his own bootstraps, and on having ended up owing only a minimum of favors.

It was after completing high school that he took a job at João Baptista, Ltd., but as an accountant, spared the exhaustion of going from one end of S. Vicente to the other delivering messages. But it wasn't long before he realized the importance of the relationships established during the previous four years. Because he knew all the businessmen on the harbor, all the boatmen and customs officers and policemen, and soon Sr. Baptista began to send Araújo whenever it was necessary to pretend to load merchandise from the customshouse while leaving it on land, since Araújo was the one who knew who would turn a blind eye and for how much, who was incorruptible (or simply mean), and at first he had participated only out of love of the firm and for the pleasure of cheating the State because he didn't see why you should pay taxes for something to enter the country. But afterward he saw that he was taking a personal risk in order to enrich his boss and he demanded a cut of the profits.

Almost from the very beginning he did the work of an assistant manager without ever having been given the job. But, as

Sr. Baptista said, he was the only one of his employees with a head on his shoulders. For example, it was Araújo who gave him the idea of sending Christmas cards to important people on the island, accompanied, of course, by crates of champagne or whiskey, depending on the status of the person, always with wishes for the greatest prosperity for Your Excellency and Your Esteemed Family. And those who didn't merit boxes of anything but who were still useful to the firm received a sealed envelope at the end of the year, all on the advice of Araújo. Thus, little by little, Sr. Baptista began to delegate authority to him, and whenever he went away he always said loudly enough that everyone could hear, If anything comes up Araújo will deal with it.

After three years at João Baptista, Sr. Napumoceno began to build his house. At that time, Alto de Mira-Mar was still a wide open space no one wanted, but Sr. Napumoceno saw how beautiful it would be to have the bay in front, even if getting up there meant a tough climb. One day I'll have a car, he thought. He would leave work at noon and run to the construction site to argue with the bricklayers. In those days blueprints and calculations were not required, everything was done freehand or to the owner's specifications, and he made a point of having the house stand out from the open space. So, for once making an exception in his choice of color, he painted the house red on the outside, but the three rooms, the porch, and the enormous living room and even the small entrance hall were all painted green.

It was after moving to the new house that Sr. Napumoceno began to think it was too big for a single man and though the outlines were still somewhat vague, he warmed to the idea of a family, a woman like Dona Rosa at the door smiling and wait-

ing for him when he got back tired from work, little ones trip-
ping over his feet. He had long since passed 30, he felt himself
to be at the prime age for settling down, and there was lots to
choose from. Up until then he'd never had a steady girlfriend,
just a few flirtations here and there, but nothing serious. Once
he'd become a little more attached than usual to a girl, at first
only as a friend, he liked being with her and talking and they
sometimes went out, but as friends. He liked visiting her home
and he used to spend hours in the parlor, the mother in the
kitchen or in the bedroom, the two of them telling jokes and
laughing. And little by little he began to make himself at home
in her house, he would go through the yard if he arrived and
she wasn't there, but he didn't think he wanted her to be his
girlfriend, just that he wanted her company, and sometimes
they would even meet on the Rua de Lisboa as he left work
and he would walk her home. And little by little he began to
find that Armanda was not just a pretty girl but also that she
seemed like she'd be the perfect companion, thoughtful as she
was, always at home, not interested in parties or flirting. But,
given the point at which they'd arrived in their friendship it
was difficult for him to ask her to go steady without being entirely sure of his intentions and so he kept putting off asking
her, in any event he was in no hurry, and she didn't seem to be
either. But, after two months of these almost daily visits, he arrived one day and not seeing Armanda went through the yard.
But instead of Armanda he found Nha Nizinha, the mother,
who barely replied to his good evening and with no preamble
abruptly said she needed to know what was going on between
him and her daughter because people were beginning to talk.
He stood there with his mouth hanging open, floored, he

hadn't expected anything like this, and since he didn't say anything Nha Nizinha thought she would help him out by adding
that people were already saying that the two were going steady
and yet she knew nothing about it. Sr. Napumoceno later
wrote, when he recounted this episode from his life in his will,
that he had no doubt he'd been enlightened by a ray from the
Holy Spirit. Because, at that deadly serious hour, he realized
right away that Nha Nizinha wanted to force him to decide
something that he hadn't yet decided. He saw that she wasn't
asking in order to find out and then object, but with the simple
goal of making the romance official, of making him tell the
family, even of being proclaimed as the fiancée. He said that at
that instant he saw himself in coat and tie, on the way to the
Justice of the Peace, Armanda dressed in white with a bouquet,
and thought, this is one of those things you decide for yourself,
without outside interference. And he surprised himself by re-
plying to Nha Nizinha with the truth, There's nothing between us, we're just friends. Nha Nizinha seemed not to be
counting on such a simple answer and for a moment she was
stunned, incredulous, but she rallied, saying that the two had
been seen in the Praça Estrela and other places; she knew that
they went out together, how was it they were only friends?
And though he insisted nonetheless that they were only
friends, Nha Nizinha said, If it's just friendship, then do me a
favor and come less often to the house, leave my little girl in
peace because people are talking. Sr. Napumoceno had no
choice but to agree politely. He said that maybe she was right,
it was true that he was coming to the house too often, he'd
avoid it in the future. Because, he shyly explained, he didn't yet
feel he had the means to be an official suitor, he was just a

simple office clerk, with no guaranteed future. But even Armanda didn't understand. When they met, she accused him of not having serious intentions, because, she said, if he had he would have told her mother he liked her. And he wasn't able to tell her that it wasn't a question of seriousness but of the way in which the situation had been put to him that had scared him off.

And until he moved to that big house he didn't give another thought to having a family, after all women are a nuisance, they all want the same thing: to lead a man to City Hall and then to the altar. But having moved, he began to feel the weight of his solitude, and yet also a certain laziness about coming down from the hilltop; he'd put on a few pounds and it was getting difficult to make the climb. So he'd arrive home exhausted from work and from the walk up and he would sit in the living room which was still sparsely furnished or else in the canvas chair that he'd placed on the porch thinking he needed a woman, but making no move to find one. And in that daily rhythm years and more years passed, with him always saying to himself that he needed to marry, but he settled in alone and didn't marry, and he met Dona Joia and made up his mind too late and so he did nothing because meanwhile he was occupied with other matters. Until one day he was struck right in the solar plexus in the middle of his firm's offices by a girl whom he'd never seen before or if he had seen her he hadn't noticed her. All that he could be sure of was that she came in and by chance he was there and he fixed the eyes of a tamed bull on her and stood rooted to the floor, his mouth open, forgetting what he'd been trying to do, and she noticed and smiled and that smile cut through Sr. Napumoceno's heart and so he approached her but was barely able to utter, Have you been helped, do you need something? And she smiled at him again, said, Thank you, I have been, but he continued standing there in front of her and she raised her eyes and he said they were the eyes of a wild gazelle because even though he would never in his life see the eyes of a gazelle he said he felt that they couldn't be different from hers, because what he saw was a veritable gazelle in her person, in her small face, in her wild eyes, in her attenuated, long-legged body, but what enchanted him most were those eyes which never stopped moving as if always afraid or surprised, and he later noticed that she didn't have any meat on her bones, but he only noticed that later because on that day and the days that followed he was completely caught up in that skinny girl who attracted him more than anything in the world and so he didn't know what else to say to her and they stood looking at each other, she smiling shyly, and then saying, Well, then, good afternoon, and preparing to leave. But with an effort he managed to say, Just tell me your name! And she heard the urgency of the plea in the voice of that man standing before her as if he'd been stunned by a blow to the head and she said softly, Adélia, smiling. Tell me where I can find you, and she, already smiling coyly, said that she was always around and left, and he didn't try to hold her back, he knew he'd anchored his destiny and he didn't feel happy, on the contrary, a profound anguish seized him because it was as if he knew that he'd have to break through a stone wall with his head and he moved toward the door and saw her rounding the corner of the market and climbing up Monte and so he left and took the Rua do Matadouro Velho, turned and almost ran through the Rua da Praia, rounded the Caizinho on the left and met up with

Adélia as he approached the Praça Estrela. He forced a smile, his heart was in his throat from the effort and the emotion, and floundering he said, It seems we have something to give one another, and she smiled with those wild gazelle eyes and said, It seems you have something to give me, and he became silent, breathing through his mouth, his breath not wanting to come out, a perverse tenderness laying hold of his voice. But, with effort, he managed to ask her, Let me walk with you a little! And she again heard in his voice that strange something that she'd already sensed when he'd asked her her name and they walked a little without talking, he wanting to speak but unable to think of anything to say, he was all out of ideas, unable to talk and unable to find the words, all he felt was that trembling in his legs and he ended up saying that he felt just like a twenty-year-old, unsure if he'd said it or just thought it, he only knew that he was still walking by her side and they climbed O Monte without saying a word until she stopped in front of a door and said, This is me, and he stopped, staring at those darting eyes, a slight tremor in her voice, too, and he thought, I'll have to find a wild gazelle to see if they look alike. She said good-bye, said, See you later, enjoy your walk! But he kept staring, said, Yes, thank you, and thought that he ought to leave but remained standing there until she extended her hand and he grasped that little hand and thought I am caught in her web, and said, I don't ever want to let go! And she smiled again and withdrew her hand and went into the house and he kept on walking though he was always turning around to see if he could see her, but she didn't reappear. Some time later, on the night of her departure to be exact, she confessed that on that day she'd stood watching him through the crack in the door-way until he disappeared in the distance.

For nearly 18 months Sr. Napumoceno allowed himself to be slowly consumed by a demented passion that ended up poisoning his existence, because, when he finally acknowledged it was over, he continued to live with the dream of Adélia, since she had confessed to him that she felt very close to a man whose eyes smiled when he saw her and who treated her like an expensive doll and was sweet and good to her.

But according to the notebooks, at first Sr. Napumoceno didn't treat her like a woman. For example, it never occurred to him to kiss her, much less to take her to bed. He felt, and of this he was sure, from the first and throughout the many years that remained to him, that he loved her. But it was a love that he knew was not innocent and that at the same time had nothing carnal in it and he liked nothing better than to be next to her in the car and to sit there quietly parked without saying a word, just looking at her, and he made her into a saint, an immaculate virgin, and when she smiled and asked, What are you looking at?, he could only reply, I'm looking at you! In the end he'd confessed to her the feelings that oppressed him and took away his peace of mind; Adélia occupied his every thought, but it was an Adélia whose features he couldn't remember. When he was away from her, he never knew whether her lips were thin or full, if her hair was long or short, so when he was near her he looked at her and closed his eyes and forced himself to memorize her and thought I won't forget what she's like again, but he always did, and one day he asked her for a photograph, Give me a picture of you so I can see you when I can't see you!

And so she gave him one, but it wasn't a photograph of his Adélia, he didn't recognize her in that image, there was nothing of the fugitive girl who eluded the mind's grasp, so he hid it at the bottom of a drawer because his Adélia was someone else, maybe that photograph was of the other man's Adélia, the one she'd said was away, his Adélia was pure, chaste, and saintly even if his friend Fonseca laughed at these words, a virgin, right, only in her left ear, he'd said, take her to bed and get it over with because if she goes out with you in your car she'll go to your house and your bed and then God will help you mount her, but the truth is he never touched her even with his little finger except for that greeting on the first day, because when he stood before her he was a boy afraid to speak lest he frighten his little bird, but one day they were both sitting in the car in silence, she listening to the crickets singing, he listening to her listening to the crickets, until she disturbed the silence and said,The crickets are entertaining us and he agreed that they were, how amusing it is to hear the crickets at night and said, Ever since I left S. Nicolau I haven't heard crickets sing! But she didn't believe it, she'd said that, Yes he had, only he hadn't paid attention, he agreed, What I know for sure is that I didn't notice! I remember that when I was a boy we would go out hunting crickets under rocks, then we would put them inside a matchbox and they would think it was already nighttime and would begin to sing. Because I don't know if you know, he explained, that crickets only sing at night, they say it's to help the night in its silence otherwise the sun doesn't know which direction to face in the morning for dawn. She laughed and said she'd never heard that, but he confirmed it very seriously. Crickets sing to guide people, but poor things, more often than not they disorient us because they all sing at the same time, each one pulling you toward it, no one can find his way in the midst of that cacophony of calls. She laughed, called him a silly, and he also laughed, and their hands met though they hadn't sought each other out and they surprised themselves at the gesture and their hands became suddenly moist, each was overcome by modesty and he let go and took out a cigarette and began to speak of his childhood in S. Nicolau, but almost forty years had gone by and he was no longer sure of the truth of what he said, if everything he remembered had really existed, but he did remember and recounted an event that he said he'd witnessed (without knowing for sure if he'd really witnessed it or simply heard tell of it), but he said that when he was still a little boy a neighbor had given birth to a child with a caul, Adélia didn't know what a child with a caul was and he explained that a child with a caul is the kind who is born in a sack and everyone knows that witches prefer to eat children in sacks because they have softer and tastier flesh, and it so happened that nearby lived a woman from Praia Branca who had the reputation of being a witch and when they saw that child so white and fat, who smiled when he was removed from the sack and was born with his eyes open, all the friends and neighbors immediately began to exorcise him, to curse the evil eye, to throw salt over their shoulders, all with the intent of protecting the child who looked like an angel fallen from heaven, but nonetheless, a few days later he began to waste away, to refuse his mother's milk, and so the midwife ordered that he be given tea of lizard's tail which was an effective antidote to spells and they put little branches of sweet marjoram under his pillow, and anointed him with goat fat, but on the

seventh day he died anyway, and when they were dressing him
for burial they found that he had a line that went from one ear
to the other on his little head, and that that line was a sure sign
that the little boy had had a hex put on him and had been eaten
by a witch, so the people were roused and ran to the house of
the woman in Praia Branca and began an exorcism, saying that
she had eaten a person's child, they shouted at her to come outside, So that we can cut off your tail, you damned witch, but
she didn't respond, she kept her door closed, then someone had
the idea of throwing a stone at the door and so everyone else
started throwing stones at the door and the windows and
shouting, You shameless witch, so the woman appeared at the
door, and he still remembered her horrified expression, staring
wide-eyed as if her eyes would jump out of her head which was
wrapped in a kerchief, a black shawl sliding off her shoulders,
and she remained standing at the door unable to say a word,
just trembling like green cane. Once she came to the door the
screams stopped as if her face had terrified all those present,
but there was one person who dared to gather another stone
that hit the door above her head and so other stones flew, and
she covered her face with her hands and she tried to go back
inside and close her door, she still wasn't saying anything, she
didn't speak or defend herself, she just stood in the doorway
staring, and it was then that everyone ran into the house. He,
Napumoceno, remained outside and so all he saw was the furniture being thrown into the street, a suitcase, bed linens, a
mattress that tore and spilled straw all over the road, plates and
chairs that broke on the stones, until Nho Jonsinho arrived
out-of-breath, shouting, In the name of the law! He was the
chief of police, people began to leave in small groups, Nho Jon-

sinho only shouted, In the name of the law, and people left, and he found the woman and dragged her into the street and gave her little slaps and he tried to open her eyes to see her pupils and he picked up a bit of mirror that had shattered in the street and then shook his head and said loudly, You've already killed the poor creature.

While Sr. Napumoceno spoke, Adélia, seeking a more comfortable position, ended up leaning on his shoulder, but he didn't even notice, and now that he was silent continued to be unaware of her playing with his fingers because he kept seeing the figure of Nha Barbara at the door, white, wrinkled, her black shawl fallen at her feet, her terrified eyes and so he didn't hear right away when Adélia said abruptly, I want to go see your house! Especially because after his conversation with Fonseca he'd said to her one day, Come to my house! and she'd reacted in a way he hadn't expected, I'll never go to your house! and so he never pursued it because he felt happy just seeing her, being with her in the car listening to the crickets. It's enough for me to know you exist, that I can see you, and every day that I see you I feel happy to know that you aren't merely a dream but the dream of my life. He said these things and then he forgot because he didn't think about them, he didn't prepare the words that he said to her, so when she would later remind him that he'd even said that she was the dream of his life, he didn't remember any of it, I'm not saying I didn't say it, but the truth is that I don't remember having said that even if those are very pretty words, he said, smiling uneasily because by then he no longer knew what to do with this love that by day tortured him and enslaved him with the desire to see her, but that at night wearied him at her side. And that very first night when

he took Adélia to his house, to his mind it was as if they were
still in the car, she, a virgin, pure, immaculate . . . They're all
whores, Fonseca had said, and in fact he discovered another
Adélia, lascivious and voluptuous, rubbing against him when
they were barely inside the door, Don't turn on the light! But
the Adélia he loved was the Adélia he'd already lost, the child
he'd seen in her, pure and innocent, the small, darting eyes always surprised, and he could still see Nha Barbara in that
doorway of his childhood, he'd taken off running, arrived home
sobbing, since no one was home he'd huddled in a corner crying, Nha Barbara still there before his eyes, but a little later
he'd heard his father and mother arriving, Serves her right,
they were saying, She had no business eating human babies!,
Now she's got her just deserts!, Adélia hanging from his mouth
while his father was taken prisoner, Adélia kissing him as his
father hugged his wife and children to say goodbye, and Nha
Barbara opened her mouth and he saw that she was missing a
lot of teeth, Mommy, what does a witch's mouth look like? But
his mother said that such questions were not for the mouths of
babes and he hugged Adélia and she bent double and he bent
double over her on the rug in the large room feeling that he
was breaking something sacred, it was as if he were breaking a
beloved object on purpose, she simply purred, still shy, only
later would she give free rein to that wild and unbridled sensuality, *don't pull out now!* she would later say when all decorum
and shyness had vanished and he was simply forcing himself to
be a man and to forget the quasi-tragedy of that first night because she was already panting and all he could see was Nha
Barbara, his mother laughing, his father laughing. *Life is a
naked woman lying on a bed*, he'd read that, he no longer re-

membered where, and he had accepted this assertion as the un-
questionable truth and for that reason he had a morbid fear of
being impotent with a woman and so they began to meet more
and more rarely, at first it was every day, then every other day,
then every two days, but when he hadn't shown up for three
days she came and knocked on his door, I was worried you
were sick, he made excuses—too much work, feeling a bit
tired—she simply smiled and then it became a habit for her to
come on foot from Monte to Alto Mira-Mar, and from the verandah he would see her coming, a kind of horror gripping him
already, because she was never tired nor sated. More, more, she
begged. I want to be yours again! she begged, but many times
at the end of their session, Adélia would begin to cry, burying
her face in the pillow and crying in long, measured sobs, all he
would see was her body trembling with the jolts of her sobs.
The first time he was worried, What's wrong? Did I hurt you?
She shook her head no. Then did I offend you? She shook her
head, her face covered by her hands because he'd forced her to
turn around. Then what is it? Nothing, it's nothing! Until he
ended up getting used to that particular complement to intercourse, and while she cried, he'd light a cigarette.

But one night Adélia arrived and announced that "he" was
arriving the following day. They'd never spoken of "him" again,
Sr. Napumoceno thought that "he" was already dead to her and
so he already felt like lord and master of her body, the propri-
etor of the flesh that his wild gazelle hid, and he'd run his hand
over her, pausing at length on her bottom or on her breasts and
would kiss her belly button saying that it looked like a flower in
bloom and she would smile and trace his forehead with her finger in a caress that ran down his ears, passed over his lips and

his neck and crossed his chest and his stomach and died between his legs, and so when she spoke it was as if his heart
stopped, but once the shock was over he managed to smile, to
seem strong. Then today the party's over, she nodded yes, and
one by one he saw the tears spring from those eyes that seemed
to speak, saw them run down Adélia's face, but he swallowed
his hurt and his jealousy, he simply wished at that moment that
the ship in which *he* was arriving would sink or that *he* would
fall in the ocean and drown, but he said softly, Stay with me!
She didn't shake her head no, he said, Marry me! and grabbed
her hand and kissed it and said to her, I don't want to lose you!
Feeling like an owner who had been dispossessed, defrauded,
outraged, Stay here and live with me! But she shook her head,
No, no I can't, and he felt sick to his stomach and he breathed
in the air that seemed to suffocate him and said, Then go! But
she didn't move, she said, I came to say goodbye to you! And
he said, We already said good-bye and she said, Like this? And
he answered, Yes, like this! And she said, Then good-bye! and
went down the steps of the verandah and he remained standing
there waiting for her to turn around, but she didn't turn around
and he wanted to call to her to come back but he didn't and she
descended the path that he'd had paved and was lost in the
night and he sat in the canvas chair and shed all the tears of the
agony of no longer having her, of no longer clasping her in his
arms, of never again seeing her naked and provocative, and all
night that unhappiness kept him prostrate in his chair because
he already saw her in the arms of that other man whom he
didn't know but hated from the bottom of his heart and remembered again her sighs and the words that she'd said and all
through the night called her at the bottom of a bottle and the

following morning he went in search of his friend Fonseca, but Fonseca didn't understand his pain, he simply said, laughing, You took, now you're taken—and now the owner comes back and claims his property. That's how it goes! But he couldn't see the humor in that, and he went away and began to see Adélia in all the women he passed; he felt as if he'd go crazy, obsessed as he was. Adélia, Adélia, where are you that you don't come, don't you see that without you I don't have any peace, don't you miss me as I miss you, Adélia my life and my dream, have you already forgotten how much fun we had together? Come, Adélia, come and slake the thirst in my mouth, come again and stick your fingers in my belly button.

But Adélia remained deaf to all appeals and Sr. Napumoceno suffered his pain alone because as he later said, We can lament another's sorrow, but no one, no one can live ours. And it was in the middle of that agony that assailed him that he returned to his childhood and remembered a place called Ribeira da Prata which he hadn't seen for more than thirty years.

## CHAPTER 6

The eighth chapter of Sr. Napumoceno's last will and testament was devoted exclusively to his vacation on S. Nicolau. He used the occasion to compose a sort of guide to the places worth visiting and even talked a little about the history of the discovery and colonization of the island, about the first families to stake a claim there, and a few of the local curiosities, namely, possible explanations for the *rotcha s'cribida*, the hieroglyphic rock, and for why the people of Praia Branca were all accused of being witches. But after little more than a month, he concluded that he was cured of the sentimental upheavals that had led him to seek out the haunts of his youth and he decided to return, especially since the person he'd left in charge of the operations of the firm was his friend Fonseca, whom he knew to be honest and true, but to possess little knack for business.

In his will he didn't go beyond what has been related, but in the third school notebook he explained in minute detail the "sentimental upheavals" that had led him to decide to put into practice that dictum of the ancients: best to place an ocean be-

tween star-crossed lovers. And in fact, having spent that time
visiting, writing, and talking with people he hadn't seen for
many years, Adélia was transformed little by little into a vague
memory of someone he'd known and wanted but who'd died,
and so, once that time had passed, he felt he could consider
himself cured, discharge himself, and go back home. It's only
natural that the very threat of being cured would have led Sr.
Napumoceno to suggestively entitle the third notebook *The
Return of Adélia*, because hardly had he opened the door of his
house when he realized that the place was full of Adélia, of her
perfume, her smile, so full that just putting the key in the lock
he'd realized he'd been in a hurry to return. In S. Nicolau she'd
been a vague memory but now she materialized in a way that
oppressed him because in searching in his pocket for his keys
he felt her snuggled up against him, both her thin little arms
encircling his waist as if she never wanted to let go, and as he
entered the living room he saw the enormous rug where for the
first time they had made love in that uncomfortable way and
he sat down on the old canvas chair and Adélia sat on his lap
curled up as if she were losing herself in him and with his
hands on the nape of her neck he experienced the sorrowful
pleasure of having her again and saw her naked and beautiful,
her slender legs leaping around the house in dancer's steps, her
stomach pulled in where he liked to rest his hand, and he
stretched out his arms and got up to catch her, to join her to
him, but she ran away, her small eyes surprised as if she were
expecting the house to fall on her head any minute, and following her through the house he caught her, but she, laughing
with those little eyes that looked like nothing so much as narrow slits, slipped from his fingers and in the excitement of that

struggle she knocked against a door and he jumped out of his
skin with the noise, but the knocking continued, and he realized he wasn't dreaming and turned on the light because it was
already dark, and he went to open the door and it was Adélia,
smiling, abashed. He didn't remember that in order for her to
come inside he had to step out of the doorway and for a good
while they stood looking at each other because she also didn't
think to ask to come in, nor did she make any move to enter,
until a draft made her shiver and she sighed and then he leaned
her against him as he used to and hugged her and rubbed her
back to make the cold go away, only he didn't smile as he used
to, but she lost herself in him, moving her arms around his
neck, leaning her face on his neck, but he simply continued to
rub her back and felt something hot running down his neck
and realized she was crying and at that moment he felt liberated and victorious and smiled and thought *sic transit Gloria
mundi*, I can lose her without pain and so he let her cry and
continued to smile while he thought, Nothing binds me to her
anymore! He lifted her in the air as he used to and took her to
the bedroom and placed her on the bed, but it was no longer an
instinctive improvisation, because now he thought about each
gesture and he thought that he ought to kiss her and he kissed
her and he thought he ought to undress her and he did and
then he thought that he ought to possess her and he did, but it
was a possession calculated to make her moan and scream
while he smiled in the dark at her contortions and convulsions
and turned on the light to see her face and remembered the
woman from Dakar in his past and went over all the caresses
she'd taught him, including the descent to the cave, raising
himself up now and again to see her face and she had her

mouth open as if she couldn't breathe or was suffering a great pain, but she managed to hiss, Turn out the light! And he thought, It's the voice of a vicious bitch, hoarse as if she were drunk, and he felt his pride swollen and appeased and enjoyed the triumph of what he thought of as his liberation there above her, master of himself and also of her lying there, disheveled, her hair stuck to her forehead, the sweat running down her body, her eyes closed, her legs open and he looked at her as if he were seeing her for the first time because he felt that he *was* seeing her for the first time and he examined her free of all sensuality and he withdrew from her saying *sic transit Gloria mundi* and headed for the bathroom.

When he returned Adélia was still in the same position, but she heard him come in and asked him for a cigarette. He gave her a lit cigarette and prepared another for himself. And while they smoked she broke the silence to say, I came to stay with you, if you still want me. He listened and smiled and looking at Adélia leaning against the headboard with a cigarette in her hand, he searched for his wild gazelle in her while he thought about how much he'd dreamed of those words during the days of his desolation, how much he'd longed to see her come in and say as she was saying now, I came to be with you . . . And he felt that in the agony of those days he'd consumed his Adélia, he'd buried her in himself, all that remained now was the dream of Adélia, but still he hesitated for the brief moment when he saw her as he'd seen her the first time in his warehouse and then surprised himself by saying that he'd lost her more than a month ago, now it was too late. Adélia didn't understand, But on that day you wanted to marry me, you even asked me to marry you, and he felt that he was smiling ironically, That was then, now it's over. How can it be over if you liked me so much, she asked, and he felt that he wanted to lay himself bare before that woman lying there in his bed, to free himself of her in order to continue in the dream of his gazelle and he said, It was as if you'd taken a piece of me because I'd wake up at night and search for my gazelle, the piece that was missing, but it wasn't there, it had run away from me, and I searched for it without finding it and I despaired of finding it and forced myself to live without it. And now that it's shown up I feel like it can't be mine because other hands touched it, manipulated it, and it has ceased to be a piece of me, and so I don't want it anymore. But I'm here, Adélia said, drawing nearer, and I'm the same person and now I know that I want you. But he shook his head: You're different, you're no longer the same. I don't understand, Adélia said. I'm hungry, he said, and got up and went into the kitchen.

And he prepared a light meal and called to her and she came naked as she always did, but he didn't even look, he just said, Go get dressed so you don't catch cold, and she went back to the bedroom and put on a bathrobe of his and came back and sat down at the table. I waited so long for this day, she said, but he just asked her if she wanted ham and cheese because there was no bread in the house. She nodded yes and added, During that whole time I couldn't get you out of my mind for even a minute. Wouldn't you like a beer?, he asked affably, and she rose to get it from the refrigerator and he asked for one, too. It's as if I'd never been separated from you, she said, but he simply busied himself with opening the beers and she remembered and smiled and said, When you'd see me you couldn't take your eyes off of me. It was like a dream or perhaps an obsession. It was an obsession, he said, smiling. You were always looking at me as if you wanted to devour me or swallow me whole. Like I'm doing now? he smiled. No, not like you're doing now. Because it was like a dream, as if it wasn't of this world. One afternoon I received a note from you. I was alone at home, someone knocked on the door . . . It was the day right after we'd bumped into each other in the square and you said that one of us had something to give the other. So, they knocked on the door and when I went to open it they gave me an envelope from Sr. Araújo. I still remember the note: After all, it did no good to try and attract you with telepathic currents, but the truth is that I wanted to see you so much that I ended up believing you were waiting for me in the office. I continue to feel your absence painfully as if a part of me had been amputated and what I want is to be with you looking into your gazelle eyes . . . Adélia, Sr. Napumoceno almost shouted. I never wrote that note! I would never write that kind of nonsense! But Adélia smiled and said, Never mind! And her voice was sweet and tender as she looked at the beer in the glass but didn't drink it.

However, she raised her eyes to him and almost anxiously asked, Isn't it a pretty little note? Remember, you're the only one who ever called me a wild gazelle! And in a playful moment she insisted, Don't you wish you had written it for me? Maybe, he smiled. Except that I never wrote it and I never knew anything about it until you started talking about it. But she smiled, a smile that faded on her lips, forgetting the ham and cheese, and suddenly she grabbed his hand and with her bird eyes bright with tears she asked if he didn't wish he'd written it for her—Don't you wish you'd written it for me?—she insisted and forced herself to smile but there was a painful anxiety in her voice while she asked, Don't you wish you'd written it for me? And her sobs rose from her throat and she squeezed his hand and said, Write it for me! And he looked stupefied at those tears that fell between smiles and he didn't know what to do or what to say and so he drew her to him and said, I already wrote it for you! Feeling in himself the anguish of those smiling tears that weighed on his heart, he repeated, I already wrote it for you! while he wiped her face and thought that he'd been with her for almost two years without knowing her because at first all he'd wanted was the ecstasy of contemplating her and then he'd been preoccupied only with that lascivious doll's body which transfixed him with the perpetual horror of falling short, but Adélia remembered the first time that he'd invited her to dinner and said, I remember it perfectly, we had dinner, the two of us, in this room by candlelight because you'd turned out the light and lit a candle, and he wanted to interrupt her and say it wasn't exactly like that, it was because the light had gone out that he'd lit the candle, but he saw there'd be no point, she wouldn't hear him because it was as if she were lost in the dream of a world he'd never seen. You looked at me in the light of that red candle and I looked at you and I felt loved and protected and happy and I didn't want to think about anything else and you weren't saying anything, but we stopped eating and kept looking at each other without saying a word and then you stretched out your hand and played with my finger . . . He remembered and smiled and accidentally said, And you asked me what that painting there meant, she didn't even look, it was simply to say something, she knew perfectly well it depicted Christ's Last Supper, but she merely asked the question to break the silence. There wasn't even any music! he said. There was no electricity, she said, then we got up from the table and went to the sofa, but he interrupted almost harshly, That happened a long time ago, and it happened to us, why tell ourselves the story! But she asked, quietly, almost somnolently, Let me relive that night once more, maybe I'm telling it my way, but that's how it was for me. And he gave up interrupting her even if her words made him feel sick and impatient because she stripped him bare before himself. He wanted that night simply to have been a night like any other in his past and so when she said On that sofa you said you loved me, he almost screamed, You're lying! But then he smiled, and said, Maybe I said I liked you a lot! Or that I liked being with you. But she repeated, You said you loved me and you kissed the palm of my hand and then you kissed my mouth and while you undressed me you said that fortunately the first time was already long past and smiling you said there is nothing more challenging for a man than the first time he makes love to a woman because he knows he is proving himself and it is always an anguished encounter because he has a horror of weakening in the midst of that affirmation and so he usually weakens and rarely is the encounter unforgettable.

aria da Graça was sorry that Sr. Napumoceno hadn't dated his notebooks because it was only from the shaky handwriting that she could tell these pages had been written at about the same time as the last part of the will. The truth was that she preferred to date the third notebook to that time period, with the sole aim of justifying her father, of believing that he'd written what he'd dreamed, not what had really happened. Because well before she'd found the notebooks she'd already come across the name Adélia among the legatees, to whom the book *Alone* by António Nobre was to be given. Moreover, and in truth, it should be stated up front that this legacy was never bequeathed, because Sr. Américo Fonseca, charged by Graça with fulfilling her father's wishes as scrupulously as possible, came up against the harsh reality of being unable to determine Adélia's whereabouts even though he'd searched all of Monte house to house, no one had been able to tell him of an Adélia who had known Sr. Napumoceno. So its delivery remained suspended—Sr. Fonseca had other obligations to fulfill—until Graça's search led her to the notebooks. At that point she became interested in Adélia's fate, she wasn't simply someone in her father's life, and she even began to think that Adélia was the person who could shed light on just who that man really was who had sired her on an office desk. But the will was very laconic on the subject, it merely said, *For Adélia, living in Monte, in this city, my book* Alone, *by António Nobre,* and it was with notebook in hand that Graça again sought out Sr. Fonseca, I'm sorry, Sr. Fonseca, but we have to find Adélia no matter what, I would be grateful if you would take another look through Monte or in other neighborhoods, we can't come to a deadlock over a book. Sr. Fonseca again set out, he wandered the outskirts of the city, trying to find out who knew Adélia, but no one was able to give him any useful information that would lead him to Adélia; some shook their heads, no, never heard of her, others pointed to people, oh, she must be the one who lives behind Sentina! but it wasn't her, and then they spoke of one Adélia, daughter of Nha Crisanta, who had a little house next to Chã de Cemitério and so he went and before him appeared a woman of 50, already old and toothless, she was Adélia de Crisanta, mother of six, all of whom had left the country, all having forgotten who'd given birth to them, no wonder they say there's no ingrate like the child of a Cape Verdean! A book? Why would the deceased have left her a book! At least if he'd left her something else, a little money perhaps, but a book! No, no it couldn't be meant for her. Besides, she'd never met any Napumoceno da Silva Araújo. Such a strange name, she wouldn't have forgotten it. She was sure the book wasn't for her nor did she need any books. For other things, yes, she was at his service! Sr. Fonseca thanked God that she wasn't the deceased's

Adélia, even though smiling with her toothless mouth she'd
said it wasn't worth searching, she was the only Adélia in S. Vicente. So just to ease his conscience Sr. Fonseca decided to
summon Adélia with an announcement on the Voice of São
Vicente. But it wasn't easy to come up with an ad that would
be clear to the interested party without compromising the reputation of the deceased. Because though the man never gave
the name of the girl over whom he'd lost his head, he had no
doubt that it was the same one whose "owner's" return had so
disoriented the deceased that his only refuge was in the shad-
ows of his past. He smiled thinking of how the city would be
scandalized the day someone mounted an inquiry into the
moral life of the petty bourgeoisie of S. Vicente and discovered
all the shamelessness it hid. For instance, he couldn't help smiling when he heard Carlos talk of his uncle's chastity because he
was privately remembering that dreamy night the deceased
had recounted having spent with the woman from Dakar,
the *descendre à cave*, and the subsequent venereal disease cured
with "914." No matter that the deceased had never said anything to him about the nights with Adélia or that Graça had
never even mentioned the contents of the notebooks, it was
plain to see that Adélia was another of the rascal's mistresses
and he, meanwhile, looking as if butter wouldn't melt in his
mouth. Because, taking things at face value, who would have
thought that that serious man, absorbed in his books, a member of the city council with ambitions for its presidency, would
be able to mount a cleaning woman on an office desk? If
Napumoceno hadn't confessed it himself, he, Fonseca, would
never have believed such foolery, especially because after getting burned with a case of gonorrhea the man had cooled

down, and concerned himself only with his business, his Sporting Club, and his City Council. And for that reason he couldn't place an ad asking for information on some Adélia who'd been lovey-dovey with the deceased Araújo going on thirty years ago, it would be the same as detonating a bomb in the city, so he opted for a sort of incommunicado: The illustrious deceased, Napumoceno da Silva Araújo, who almost a month ago abandoned us to the irreparable pain of his departure, left many of his personal belongings to several citizens in this city, which he loved as if it were his birthplace. Almost all those people have been located and the various legacies dutifully handed over for the perpetuation of the memory of our friend, who is sorely missed and mourned and irrevocably gone. But until now we have not been able to find the address of one of his childhood friends, a woman by the name of Adélia, to whom he left a valuable memento. So we ask that her Excellency, Dona Adélia, please contact us at the offices of Araújo, Ltd., to receive into her possession the object that . . .

Though the communication was broadcast for six days, three times a day, Adélia did not show up, and so Maria da Graça took it upon herself to look in every nook and cranny until she discovered the whereabouts of her father's great love or definitively concluded that Adélia did not exist except in the old man's imagination. The third notebook in particular seemed to her rather exotic and she would have been tempted to allow that all of it might have been invented were it not for the statement in the will that it was after his first return from S. Nicolau that he understood that life can amount to more than worrying about earning money and that he devoted himself to foolish things like becoming an amateur photographer, then a landscape painter—there were still canvases of his at home depicting Mount Cara and the bay and other views of the city—and lastly, already at the end of his life, that he had missed his true calling which was, in the end, to be a writer. And on reams of ruled foolscap, dutifully filed in cardboard folders, Graça found the old man's notes on the great flood, in which he'd recorded how he'd brought the rain with his umbrellas and his impressions of that terrible disaster. In fact it was thanks to him that Graça ended up with a better idea of the extent of that tragedy she'd heard tell of since childhood. Because Sr. Napumoceno didn't confine himself to talking of ruined houses or of abstract people shivering with cold in the street and crying out in their impotence. On the contrary, he spoke of people whom he'd actually known and who were suddenly desperate. He spoke, for instance, of a Nha Rosa in whose house he'd been and whom he'd found balancing on the partition that divided the living room from the bedroom, holding onto the ceiling beams with one hand and onto a child with the other. I saw straightaway that she wasn't right in the head because the water had already emptied from the house and still Nha Rosa stood on the partition. I called out to her, Nha Rosa, Nha Rosa, but she didn't move from where she was, as if the two of them were dead. The waters had shifted the furniture—the mattress and the clothing and even the suitcase were soaking wet. I was led to conclude that the water had come crashing in, but that luckily the door to the kitchen garden had given way in the end and the water had emptied out through there. Nha Rosa stayed on the partition until I got on a table to take the child from her grasp. But she looked as if her other hand had been welded to the two-by-four she was holding onto and only with a lot of difficulty was I able to pry her loose, since only her eyes, fixed in terror, responded to my calls.

Reading here and there, Graça flipped through all the papers of the deceased and on scattered pages she found various complements to the will, namely, certain impressions of S. Nicolau, a full account of his vacations in Boa Vista, from which Sr. Napumoceno had surely extracted what he had thought worthy of being included in the will, because beyond small corrections in the language, the text was the same, with the omission of a small scene that had occurred between him and Dona Joia when they returned from the party in Rabil. On that night he was already in bed when he heard a light knock on the door, so light in fact that he thought he'd left the door to his room open. Afraid, as he'd been all his life, of drafts, he hurried to get up and close the door when the knock came again. He opened it to see what was going on and in front of him appeared a white figure which he recognized as Dona Joia. Now, a lamentable thing occurred. He'd forgotten to pack pajamas and so he found himself standing in his drawers in front of a woman whom he considered to be of the best society. He wanted to hide behind the door and he was about to open his mouth to beg her pardon when Dona Joia placed her mouth squarely on his in a kiss that would surely have been tender had he been prepared to receive it. Because while it lasted, all he could think about was the hurry he'd been in to take off his pants and go to bed and of the sad figure he cut wearing drawers down to his knees in front of a lady. It didn't actually occur to him that the lady might want to come in and he did nothing to make that possible. So when they heard a cough at the end of the corridor, Dona Joia ran to her room and the following

morning she returned to being the same person as before,
Good morning, dear Sr. Araújo, did you sleep well? I hope you
have a safe trip and don't forget the friends you've made in Boa
Vista.

On Adélia, however, Sr. Napumoceno produced nothing
more and this seemed particularly strange to Graça. So, she
proceeded to investigate discretely around Monte and visited
various "houses" in that area. It so happened that in all of the
ones she entered Sr. Napumoceno was not unknown. A man of
great fortune and great wisdom, they told her. Very compli-
mentary too, always calling everyone by name. Of course, they
hadn't seen him for years. They'd heard he was ill, old age
spares no one. But a very good man. On Adélia, however, no
information. The oldest spoke indeed of an Adélia who'd disappeared long ago from Monte, no one knew where to. Yes, a
skinny girl, always smiling and wide-eyed. It had been years
since they'd seen her around. Had she emigrated? Could be!
Especially since her boyfriend was an emigrant. But if she'd
gotten married, they would have known, right? Had Sr. Araújo
come around? Yes, at the beginning, when he'd first ordered
the car, he'd pass by in that flashy vehicle, the prettiest and
cleanest car in S. Vicente, we didn't even dare touch it. But
then he'd stopped coming, probably he'd started frequenting
other locales. And so it went, from one place to the next, Graça
searching Monte and then Monte Sossego. And she finally
thought of asking her mother who this Adélia might be, to
whom Sr. Napumoceno had left a memento. But her mother
could only suggest that it might have been some nurse who'd
come to give him a shot.

Graça couldn't make up her mind to move to Alto Mira-

Mar once and for all, but the truth was she was already spending all her time there among the deceased's papers and combing through his belongings. And that was how one day, inside a drawer in the closet, she found a leather zippered briefcase which was locked and sealed with wax and to which was affixed a note that read *For my daughter Maria da Graça with all her father's love.* She held it in her hands for a moment until she realized she was afraid of the revelations she would find there. Then she decided to break the seal and open it and empty its contents, but, besides poems and chronicles of the trips that he'd taken for three months, she found nothing. She looked in vain for something that would in one form or another lead her to Adélia and flipping through she found a reference to Carlos. She pulled out the relevant paper and in this way came to know the profound reasons that had led Sr. Napumoceno to strike Carlos from the roster of those he considered family. The text was, however, almost pathetic, because, as if he stood before a jury, Sr. Napumoceno justified each step of his conduct at the same time as he investigated in great detail Carlos's every word and gesture to lend support to his verdict. To introduce Graça to the issue, he said that there was no doubt in his mind that Carlos had not looked kindly on his return from vacation. To begin with, over a brief period of three months, he received nothing less than eight letters from him, long letters (to which he sometimes responded with postcards from the places he was visiting), that detailed, of course, how well the firm was doing, but also seemed to suggest—between the lines—that he should travel as much as he liked, that he shouldn't hurry back, that the firm was up and running and in fact, perhaps even better off without Sr. Napumoceno. Now, having returned without actually letting anyone know of his arrival ahead of time, he found that everything was indeed in order, the debits and credits accounted for, the imports on schedule, the clients on various islands furnished with opportunities, the marketplace in S. Vicente satisfied with Carlos's amiability, and so after a summary analysis of the firm's status he opted not to interfere too much, to let the boy plow ahead and prove himself, especially because he had other concerns he considered more important. He began, however, to dislike the way Carlos had of smiling at his pursuits which once he even dared to qualify as feverish. Sr. Napumoceno wasn't sure if Carlos was referring to the feverishness of fever or to the feverishness of having a lot to do because he simply said, Uncle, you're feverish, accompanied by a smile that to him seemed mocking. Nonetheless, he called his attention to the greatness of America where it had long been known that people didn't even have time to scratch their heads, something which he'd had the opportunity to verify *in loco*. But Carlos, with what Sr. Napumoceno considered the usual arrogance of youth, replied, but we're in Cape Verde, far from America, and here we're in charge of time. In the end he was unable to understand what Carlos really meant, because in truth he didn't think of Carlos as a lazy boy, on the contrary, with him things always went as planned, with no fuss and bother. And so, the external facts provoked two strains of thought in Sr. Napumoceno: first, he concluded that he was merely tolerated in the firm that he'd created through his very own efforts; two, he ascertained that far from being loved by his nephew for whom he'd done everything, including sending him to Lisbon to treat his tuberculosis, Carlos in fact only wished for his death so that he could begin luxurating in a fortune that he'd find was already firmly consolidated—perhaps he would even forget to have a mass said at least once a year for the eternal rest of his uncle who'd spent his life slaving and scrimping for him. And with these bitter thoughts, Sr. Napumoceno had to admit that after all Carlos showed no respect, friendship, or consideration at all, and was anxious simply for him to die quickly and inexpensively. He recalled, for example, Carlos's glee the day that he, Napumoceno, had declared that there were other presidents besides the President of the Republic, that even amongst ourselves there was the City Council President. Because with him in the City Council, preoccupied with municipal concerns, Carlos would be the sole and exclusive head of the firm Araújo, Ltd., doing and undoing at will, without having to ask for permission. And in the days that followed it seemed to him that when Carlos would come to his office he was more ingratiating than ever, more servile even, busy leaving little written messages like I hope you slept well or, when they met, Good morning dear uncle, still going strong, hunh? But in truth it was as if he wanted to hear in reply, No, my nephew, things are bad, I can no longer drag this old carcass around, and in fact, one day when he'd purposely stayed away from work, Carlos showed up at his house, breathless. What a shock he'd had when Sr. Napumoceno opened the door, I'm fine, I just wanted to sort through some papers.

It so happened, however, that on the next day he got to his office and immediately turned the answering machine on to see what messages might have been left him. True, he was rarely disturbed, he'd never been a man for bureaucracy, his accounting system was credit/debit, and with Carlos handling imports, he'd devoted himself exclusively to study, to preparing himself to write his life story as a *self-made man* in order to show coming generations that only productive work linked to a basic education can free a man from darkness and misery. But even so, every day he turned on the answering machine, more out of habit than in hopes of finding a message. And on that day he turned it on and heard: You are nothing but a worn-out old man, you are convinced that people don't know that you made your fortune running contraband and robbing old Baptista blind when he was already gaga, you came from São Nicolau with your flea-bitten feet and now you're the fine gentleman but a lot of people still remember you with your hand on the plow in Praia Branca scaring crows away during the wet season and even here in S. Vicente delivering messages for Coré, you quickly forgot you'd been a nobody but someday someone will come along with the courage to take you down a peg and make you remember a few things.

Sr. Napumoceno heard that speech from beginning to end, as much from feeling he didn't have the strength to unplug the machine as from wanting to hear it. And when the machine was quiet he felt like throwing it to the floor and crushing the son of a bitch who'd defamed him for no reason, as if it were shameful to have risen in life through his own efforts, without owing anybody anything, by dint of his own work and his own intelligence. It was my own hard work! he yelled, and Carlos showed up at the door, smiling helpfully, and said, Uncle? But seeing Sr. Napumoceno's apoplectic face he inquired with concern whether he wasn't feeling well. What's wrong? Did something happen? But Sr. Napumoceno had pulled himself to-

gether, It's nothing, I felt ill but it's over now, you can go back
to work, I probably had too much coffee.

Carlos paused another moment, looking at his uncle, looking around, ready to be of service or call for help in case help
were needed, but seeing that the attack had passed that cynical
smile unadvisedly crossed his face again and he retired, wishing
his uncle a speedy recovery.

Sr. Napumoceno rose and paced around his office, at first
with large strides, his head held high and his hands dangling,
then in small steps, his hands behind his back and his chin
tucked into his chest. But as he paced back and forth he had
the feeling that he wasn't alone. And he noticed that the chink
of light that normally pooled beneath the door was not making
its presence known. He opened the door suddenly and Carlos
almost fell into his office, but even so Sr. Napumoceno ad-
mired the boy's sangfroid as he said, a little shaken, that he was
just about to knock, to find out if everything was okay. Sr.
Napumoceno asked angrily, Why are you spying on me? But
Carlos smiled, What an idea, uncle, I was just worried about
you, about your condition, I saw you arrive in a good mood
and then suddenly this abnormal agitation, I think you're
hiding something from me, uncle. Boy, said Sr. Napumoceno,
softening up, I'm tired of telling you that a secret must belong to one person alone and that one person is already one
too many. Two spells disaster. So you shouldn't worry about
trying to know more than you need to know. Go back to
work.

But as he closed the door again, a light bulb went on in his
brain and then more light bulbs and so he smiled, sat down,

and grabbed a pencil and paper. First: every day I have only to open the front door and there's Carlos bowing and scraping, Good morning uncle, Did you sleep well, etc., etc. Today no Carlos and yet he maintains that he saw me come in and he just declared that I'm hiding something from him. Second: as I retrace Carlos's movements from the moment he came into my office, I notice that he entered with his eyes fixed on the answering machine and he didn't take his eyes off it and as he left he was still staring at it, as if he knew that the source of my pain was the answering machine. Third: Carlos is the only person who knows that I have an answering machine because up to now he's the only one to have used it to say *Good night, uncle*. Fourth: every day he leaves a message, even if it's only a *See you tomorrow, uncle,* but yesterday he didn't. Conclusion: he was leaning against the door because he knew about the message and wanted to see how much pain he had caused me.

Sr. Napumoceno was almost smiling happily when he turned on the answering machine to listen to the message a second time. And listening he thought about what to do with that ingrate, that bastard, that son of a bitch whom he'd rescued from a life of toil and cured of tuberculosis. When his brother died, his nephew had written him a letter asking for his uncle's help. He knew of his prosperity and he, Carlos, was all alone in the world. If only he would find him a simple job as a humble servant in his store he would be forever grateful and in his debt, etc. Napumoceno concluded, after meeting his nephew, that he couldn't have been the one to write that letter, because he could see that the only thing in Carlos's head were numbers. But he'd accepted anyway; he'd wanted to make a man of him. And he gave him an education and only when he realized that unfortunately he was throwing his money out the window on schooling did he decide to get him a job. But now Carlos had forgotten everything, forgotten that he might well inherit a fortune, and had joined the slanderous scum who wanted to hold him to account for his origins. He began to write the message down and noticed that the sound was muted, as if the person were trying to disguise his voice, but in any event it was someone who didn't enunciate Portuguese properly, he said you *ur*, for you *are*, he said *fahleas* for *fleas*, and he said *S. Nincolau* and he remembered that whenever Carlos said *S. Nincolau* he always corrected it to S. *Nicolau* . . .

Once again he saw a shadow in the doorway. He said softly, You can come in, and Carlos entered, and Sr. Napumoceno stood looking at him thinking *Ungrateful world, better to cry than to pride oneself on the observation,* but he said, From this moment onward I never want to see you again, and Carlos didn't even try to deny it, he simply said, Uncle, it was just a joke, a joke in really bad taste, in fact I really like you and I know that I owe you a lot, including your having brought me from S. Nincolau, but Sr. Napumoceno was unmoved. Get out of my sight and I'll send on whatever crap you have here, and Carlos left, head bowed, embarrassed. In the afternoon, Sr. Napumoceno received a letter from Carlos but refused to open it.

He confessed, however, that he no longer felt like dealing with the tribulations of the docks, of the suppliers, of import forms, and all the rest of it. He'd spent seven years removed from those nuisances and he didn't want to deal with them again. He not only had enough to live on but he was also still committed to his writing project. So he considered liquidating the firm Araújo, Ltd., retiring from business, and living on his income. On the other hand, it hurt him to destroy what was essentially a life's work and he saw himself walking by Salina and seeing the imposing signage of ARAÚJO, LTD.—IMPORT/EXPORT replaced by any old name, that of some resaler in the trade. So he spent bitter nights meditating on the best solution, and as if the Ramireses had read his mind they offered to set up a joint venture, a project which seemed to them advantageous in every way: to create a Ramires and Araújo, Ltd.—with an initial capital investment that was neither large nor small, they'd split it 50/50—that would draw on and continue the Araújo legacy. He quickly seized upon this proposal, especially because the only conditions he placed on it—to remain in retirement and only receive dividends—were enthusiastically accepted. And it was only later that he saw the trap into which he'd fallen, the Ramireses were wholly without resources, broke, in debt up to their eyeballs, lacking even enough money to put down the initial capital.

## CHAPTER 8

*T*he leather briefcase provided Maria da Graça with an almost exhaustive picture of her father, allowing her to re-create his daily routine from dawn to dusk and to become almost as familiar with his eccentricities and habits as if she'd lived with him her whole life. She came to know for instance that Sr. Napumoceno got up every day at 6:00, whether in good or ill health. He would open the window of his room which looked out on Monte Cara and breathe in deeply thirty times, in order, as he explained, to take the pulse of the weather and the city. Afterward he'd head for the bathroom where first he'd pee, then he'd wash his hands and brush his teeth, always with American Pepsodent toothpaste. He'd brush his teeth—front, right, left, top, bottom, back—for five minutes, marking the time on the bathroom clock, and then he'd gargle letting the foam slide down his throat only to subsequently eject it, gagging. Following that, he'd switch brushes, conscientiously brushing his tongue, and only after that would he sit down on the toilet where he entertained himself reading magazines and other leaflets from a library of light reading, just right for such an elevated seat. He used four toothbrushes a day, two in the morning, one after lunch, and the fourth before going to bed, and every week he used 28 toothbrushes, each set of four in his plastic cup, each labeled according to the day of the week, each color indicating the place or the time, green for teeth, red for tongue, yellow after lunch, and blue before bed. He said he'd heard that a modern man must get used to spending at least two minutes of his 24-hour day on such important things as the hygiene of his most important organ of social contact, and so he decided that he would spend at least eight minutes a day on his mouth.

But what most impressed Maria da Graça about her father's personality was the passion that he showed for order and method. At 7:30 he would rise from the toilet for a cold shower and at 7:45 he would sit down to a breakfast of coffee and toast. At 8:00 on the dot he opened his private office for cleaning, did some work or went out on errands, and by 12:25 returned home for an aperitif before lunch. Ever since that fateful night of champagne at The Royal and the subsequent floods he'd vowed never again to set foot in a bar. But he liked to have his aperitif at home and what he drank depended on whether it was a work day, a day off, or a Sunday. On normal days he preferred dry vermouth, on days off and Sundays, it was always gin and tonic. He lunched regularly at 1:00, always alone, the maid would serve him and then retire, and right on the hour he would head for the dining room where he would chew each bite 25 times, be it meat, fish, or something else. He'd also gotten this from a book. After lunch he would linger over a *digestif*. If it was a weekday it was always *aguardente velha* de Santo Antão, on Sundays and on days off, three-star

French cognac. Only on holidays or saints' days did he allow himself five-star cognac or VSOP.

He also revealed himself to be similarly demanding in regard to his clothing, especially his whites, for which he insisted on special attention. His notorious eccentricity of only buying a suit every two years was purely financial in origin and didn't stop him from insisting on the utmost care, perfection, and attention for his underclothes. He liked, for instance, for his drawers and his undershirts to be run through blueing after they were washed to make the white brighter, but it couldn't be a blueing agent that was so light it didn't leave a shine, or so heavy it gave the clothes a blue cast. This was his principle domestic issue with the servants, and so every time he had to switch housekeepers he required that they be tested on how they prepared the blueing. He was very pleased when Dona Eduarda crossed his path and came to work for him at home. He praised her constantly, considering her a quiet, respectful, and hardworking woman, and on many separate pieces of paper Graça found phrases such as this one: I'm enchanted. Dona Eduarda prepared me a succulent steak. Or: No one can iron a shirt better than Dona Eduarda.

Thus, day by day, Graça acquired a posthumous knowledge of her father that moved her deeply and it was with sorrow that she found she had devoured the entire contents of the leather briefcase. She noticed, for instance, that for Sr. Napumoceno there was no such thing as a superfluous detail—everything that was related to his life was important and worth noting for posterity. But it was with frank emotion that she read the pages in which Sr. Napumoceno spoke of children in general and of Maria da Graça in particular. It seemed that he'd never wanted to have a child, because, he said, No matter how much you might want a child, no one knows *a priori* whether or not he is able to have one since that depends on imponderables beyond human control. Thus I find it absurd that anyone would say that he'd made a baby because he'd wanted to. But, on the other hand, making a baby is a kind of challenge to a man, because he knows that inside he has the potential to kick-start a mechanism which, it must be said, he doesn't kick-start when he chooses but when he chances to. And hence the normal desire of every man to want to know if he, too, is able to procreate since having children has been elevated to the category of individual affirmation to such a degree that I've often heard people say that someone had passed through the world as if he'd never been there because he hadn't even succeeded in having a child. However, keeping in mind the most divergent social circumstances, often what one desires is the woman, not a child by her . . .

And without a doubt he'd suffered a terrible shock when he'd learned that Maria Chica, his cleaning lady, was pregnant by him, her boss, because not only was this paternity undesired, but also impossible to acknowledge publicly. He'd thought of procuring an abortion locally but realized it would give rise to a lot of talk. So he'd opted to send her to Lisbon, it was an expense the firm was well able to afford. But Maria Chica wouldn't even hear of it. She'd always wanted a child, she'd lamented being sterile, and so now that God was giving her one she wasn't going to take it away from Him. And she remained insensible to Sr. Napumoceno's arguments about the inconvenience of the child, finishing up by saying that a child without a father was one thing there was plenty of in this world, one more wouldn't make any difference. She would gladly promise never to reveal who the father was. Faced with this good will, the firm decided to let her retire, and she moved to Lombo de Tanque and each month the firm would send her her pension.

For 25 years, Dona Chica received her pension and signed for the amounts without ever once seeking out Sr. Napumoceno for any reason whatever. From the clerk, he heard of the birth of the little girl and since Dona Chica was already living with Silvério there were no unpleasant remarks about the child's paternity. So, it was only when Maria da Graça was about to turn 12 that Sr. Napumoceno actually met her. Even though he was somewhat curious to know what the child whom he knew to be his daughter was like, he did nothing to seek her out because no concrete interest drew him to her. Above all, he felt not the slightest guilt about her birth: first, because he knew he had wanted to possess the mother and not to have a child; second, because the decision about her birth had been entirely her mother's, his advice had neither been sought nor given. And if the company thought it a good idea to award a pension to a pregnant woman who was forced to leave her job, the only thing he, Napumoceno, could do was to agree. And if that pension was periodically adjusted that was due to increases in the cost of living and not to any other special considerations.

Thus he was never able to give himself a plausible explanation of what had one day led him to the door of the high school just when classes let out. But right away he allowed himself to be dazzled by the cheerful and noisily happy sea of white smocks and remained standing there, watching that

youthful crowd and feeling a little sorry that he'd never had the
luck to experience such moments in his own life. It so happened, meanwhile, that three little girls talking loudly and
smiling at each other walked in Sr. Napumoceno's direction.
He said that when the girl in the middle looked at him it was
as if his heart were being ripped out, such were the leaps it
made, as if it were trying to jump out of his mouth. He was
sure that if at that moment someone covered his mouth he'd
certainly die because it was as if the air found all the passages
of his throat too constricted with emotion, with the secret
pride of knowing he was the father of that happy, pretty girl,
with the lively eyes, blood of his blood, who seemed to have in-
herited his intelligence, his shrewdness, and even maybe his
luck, and for the first time in his life and at that instant he took
pride in being able to say that, Yes, he was self-made and he'd
also made a baby, a child, who, he decided, would inherit his
name and his wealth. But as all those thoughts crossed his
clouded mind, the girl must have noticed his embarrassment
and smiled and said hello and he felt that an impulse, a de-
monic power was pushing him toward her and he wanted to
hug her and say, I'm your daddy, give your daddy a hug! But he
checked that impulse and simply said, Excuse me! And she
stopped in front of him and, still in a trembling voice, he was
able to ask if she was the daughter of Dona Chica. Still smiling
the girl said that she wasn't, and pointed to another girl who
was coming toward them, and called out Graça! Graça! Come
here! And Sr. Napumoceno smiled at the girl who came running, thinking he'd been fooled by the rumor of his blood.
Graça was attentive but reserved. She knew about the firm
Araújo and about her mother's pension, but she didn't know the

owner personally, though her mother had spoken many times of Sr. Araújo. So, said Sr. Napumoceno, I told your mother I wanted to be your godfather but she baptized you without telling me. Give her my compliments. She nodded and Sr. Napumoceno stood staring at that adolescent who, though his daughter, was a stranger to him. Now I hope we'll meet more often, he added, and she smiled, staring at that old man who was making his good-byes and asking for a kiss on the cheek.

Reading these pages Graça remembered the encounter and the fact that after the little old man had gotten into his car the four of them had burst out laughing saying he must be crazy. But as she read on, she saw that after all it was no coincidence that they always ran into each other at the end of each semester or after exams, What a pleasure to see my ungrateful goddaughter, how are those grades, your exams, etc., or that he always happened to have a small present for her. The first time they met she'd spoken to her mother about Sr. Araújo, but she'd only smiled and said that, Yes, he'd wanted to be her godfather. And meanwhile she said that Sr. Araújo was a good man and she could trust him. And so she never remembered to tell her about the other meetings and then she finished high school and got a job and they rarely met because she made sure to stay away from any roads that might lead her to Sr. Napumoceno, convinced as she was after she turned sixteen that he harbored libidinous intentions toward her. In fact, either he knew or he found out when her birthday was. And on that day Sr. Napumoceno made sure to run into her, not as was usual, outside the school, but in the open field between Sentina and Lombo do Tanque. Both seemed to be very surprised at the encounter and Sr. Napumoceno offered to take her home. She

declined, saying she'd get spoiled, after all he couldn't give her a
lift every day. On the contrary, he replied right away, I can perfectly well give you a lift every day. For me, being with you is a
great pleasure and it's nothing for me to come and fetch you
and bring you back. She was still smiling at these words when
he, as if he'd suddenly remembered, said, Oh that's right, you
turn sixteen today! It's a lovely age for a lovely girl like you.
The boys will be coming around, but you should run away
from them because they have no future for themselves much
less for anyone else and all they want is to have a little fun. But
you don't need them because luckily you have people who can
help you out. She smiled and asked him who, and he replied
right away, Me, for example. I brought you a birthday present
so that you can buy something pretty for yourself, he said,
handing her an envelope.

Just as she did nine years ago Graça feels the blood rush to
her face remembering that painful moment. Confronted with
that envelope a sudden rage against that dirty old man had invaded her whole body and since she was already leaning into the
car door, she'd pushed his hand away. Who do you think you are
to buy me with money?, she'd asked, furious, and only now did
she remember the shocked eyes of the old man looking at her
uncomprehendingly, he wanting to speak and she stopping him
because the words rush from her own mouth, You must know
plenty of women who take money from men, but neither I nor
anyone in my family are people of that sort! And the old man
raises both his hands and is able to say, Wait, wait, it's not what
you're thinking, it's pure friendship, with no ulterior motive, but
she keeps talking, right now she's no longer sure of his exact
words, however she remembers with shame having called him a

dishonest old man who thinks he can buy everyone with money, but she can't be bought, she's not one of those, thank God she never lacked for anything at home! But Sr. Napumoceno's eyes are red and feverish, and now she realizes that he was probably crying, and he says only, It's not what you're thinking, pulls away, and leaves her on the road. Now she wonders if she ever told her friends that the dirty old man had offered her money. She remembers that she didn't have the courage to talk to her mother about what happened, but on the night her mother got to the part about Sr. Araújo offering her 500 *escudos* she hid her head so as not to suffer the second shame of knowing that many years before when she'd said no woman in her family had ever accepted money from a man her mother had accepted money from Sr. Napumoceno.

Graça finds it strange that Sr. Napumoceno could have purely and simply forgotten that disagreeable moment and looks through his various papers to see if somewhere he made note of the incident. But just as he had with Adélia he preferred not to remember certain things, that one day his own daughter had taken him for a lecher. Because all she found were more pages in which Sr. Napumoceno spoke of his social life and certain ambitions he'd nursed over the years. He spoke again of Dr. Sousa who had opened his eyes to a friendly but superficial S. Vicente, to easy but casual and passing friendships, as if people were determined not to be labeled or to form ties. And his own experience taught him that this island changed people, made them easygoing, almost adrift, preoccupied only with making money for carousing, as if this were the only thing worth doing in life. And he ended up embarking on an analysis whose principal thesis was as follows:

S. Vicente is a recently populated island, made up of the natives of other islands whom drought, unemployment, and other miseries have forced to emigrate. Now, these people abandon islands with strong traditions, with rooted ways of being in the world, to suddenly launch themselves into a realm not only savage but also comparatively hostile and where, in order to survive, they are obliged to mix with different regional cultures and the result is that no one group has enough of a majority to dominate. And this circumstance, the absence of an ancestral link to the land, makes the man of S. Vicente light and fluid, lacking in the salutary steadfastness and firmness of the native of Santo Antão or Santiago where all regional social values remain untouched. And without a doubt it's interesting to note the loss of robustness, whether physical or mental, of these native peoples when they are placed in direct contact with S. Vicente, because they go from being individuals who are quiet, thoughtful, and careful in their choice of words to being cheap talkers always in need of affirmation. And as if that weren't enough, the population of this island, just as it began the process of forming what might have become a *sui generis* regional culture, saw itself subjected and influenced by another culture, American culture, which was not only powerful but rigid and dominating and for that very reason became the essential reference point for every resident of the island, without prejudice, certainly, to other foreign cultural forms which were constantly passing through and though less notable were no less significant. And the result of all this is that the native of S. Vicente is the most inauthentic of Cape Verdeans.

Maria da Graça smiled as she read those pages, but she thought that the old man had a point and had known how to isolate, from pure instinct, a behavior that deserved to be more carefully studied. Could it be that he considered himself a member of that rapacious group of which he spoke with such harshness or did he see himself as an exception? Indeed she noticed that Sr. Napumoceno didn't refer to particular friendships, with the exception of Dr. Sousa who, he said, had always and for his entire life honored and distinguished him with his friendship and sound advice.

As if concerned to alert his daughter to the society in which, by dint of commercial obligations, she would daily mix, Sr. Napumoceno had left inside the leather briefcase a voluminous notebook devoted exclusively to the Grémio Club in which its members were treated with particular harshness. He called the Grémio a place of perdition that began with lies and ended with prostitution. Pretending to be a gathering place for Mindelo's high society, it's nothing more, in the end, than the social intercourse of thugs in suits and ties.

After having taken the biggest misstep of his life—which was to form a partnership with the Ramireses—he was invited to become a member of the Grémio Club, doubtless through the influence of that pack of swindlers, who, being one of the oldest names in business and among the first founders of the club, were also the greatest recidivist debtors in the city, as he came to discover, sadly, too late. He blamed himself for having had faith when the first rule of a good businessman is never to have faith except in credit and debit. But he'd placed his trust in the name, as if *Ramires* could in some way bring greater luster to the honored Araújos, only to conclude that beyond the sonorous name there was nothing, not even enough money to put down an initial share of 150 *contos*. However,

what most offended him about the Ramireses was that one of
them had tried to sell him admission to the Grémio, confiding
in him, just as they were speaking of the urgent need to pro-
duce the Ramireses' share, that he was taking the necessary
steps for his admission. And this he was told with slaps on the
back and big smiles, as if it were general knowledge that he
coveted this consecration as others dream of being awarded a
medal. It was true that when he set up on his own, he'd very
rightly aspired to being admitted as a member of the Grémio
Club. Because after all S. Vicente was a city dominated by
businessmen, the Grémio their clubhouse, and he, already a
prosperous businessman whose firm was still expanding, saw
no harm whatever in belonging to a group of his peers. And in
that direction he'd made some covert attempts, no formal ap-
plications, just veiled inquiries here and there to some of the
members of that social organization, of the sort, Some day I'm
going to get to know your retreat, it seems to be a cheerful,
convivial place, S. Vicente lacks diversions, only skirts offer a
little fun, but you know, in my position I can no longer permit
myself those sorts of antics, I prefer quieter spots, etc., but the
truth is that everyone pretended not to understand, saying simply, Yes, yes, the Grémio is a nice place, a great place for a
drink, come by some time, say you're coming as my guest,
when what he wanted to hear was, Listen, man, you're already
one of us and the Grémio is yours, it's a disgrace that you're not
a member yet, I'm going to put your name up right away! But
not a single one of them did and he never dared to apply on his
own because he knew many in the trade who'd been turned
down, and the thought of that happening to him was particularly vexing. Above all else, he found hateful the way in which

new members were admitted. A fixed number of black and white balls were placed in a bag that was left in a cabinet set aside for that purpose. And the five directors, one at a time, went to the cabinet and took out a ball, which they placed in another bag. At the end the balls were counted. Three white, two black, in. Three black, two white, rejected. Now Napumoceno could never subject himself to such vexations and so he began to avoid the members of the Grémio, sometimes he would even call them a pack of cheats, many of them gave themselves airs but in the end they couldn't even lay claim to a plot in the ground. So, when through the influence of the Ramireses he was invited to be a member, he refused with gusto and a maxim from Solomon: "I considered all that my hands had done and the toil I had spent in doing it, and behold, all was vanity and a striving after wind, and there was nothing to be gained under the sun."

Maria da Graça was unable to fully explain this part of her father's life, but there seemed to her to be some bitterness in the fact that he was considered worthy of the Grémio only after he had formed an association with Ramires whom he considered decrepit when compared to a vigorous, straight-backed Araújo who didn't need the validation of uppity swindlers.

Meanwhile, Sr. Napumoceno, faced with the awkwardness of not being part of Mindelo's high society, began to replace all social interaction with the pleasures of reading. He had to confess that he couldn't quite determine when he'd acquired the vice of reading, because a bona fide vice it was, a sort of sedative opium that he took to recoup from both physical and spiritual exhaustion, and also from the annoyances of the day or the excitement of a deal. Sometimes he would fall asleep in the canvas chair, and the book would slip from his hands. But since he'd decided he needed to read at least two hours a day, until this period of time had passed he didn't retreat to his bed.

Thus, bit by bit, Maria da Graça reconstructed her father's life. She even concluded that toward the end of his life he'd also begun to be interested in Buddhist philosophy because she found passages in his texts in which he defended the merits, necessity, and utility of concentrating on and within ourselves in the search for what others call nirvana but which he preferred to call a state of pacific indolence.

But he also spoke of his term as city councilman and of the goals that had driven him. He knew people said that he'd been motivated by the vainglory of moving among the powerful men of the island, when in fact he'd accepted the job only out of the desire to serve a people and a city that had helped him to get on the straight and narrow, and out of the naïve idea that a city councilman could play a useful role in the life of the municipality. But unhappily he realized it was simply a seat at the table, the councilman was just filler to help make up the number, someone to clap, and say, Yes, sir. They were all incapable of pinpointing a problem or offering a solution. And so he resigned from the city council to prepare himself, with theoretical tools, for the job of president. He took pains to study the old traditions of the polis and was stunned to learn that the original concept of the city dated back to Roman times. For Sr. Napumoceno the president of the city council could be nothing other than the delegate of the plebeians, a defender of *civitatis*; never just another representative of the power of the State. Exactly as the Roman sages had conceived of the office, such were the aims of his presidency: roads to build, streets and highways to pave, cleaning the city from top to bottom, policing vagrancy, providing regular handouts to the needy and aid to the unemployed, beautifying the city with statues or busts of its most illustrious sons—these were all things that only a city government turned toward its people could do, occupied as the district administrator tended to be with fulfilling the governor's orders. On this matter Sr. Napumoceno had left behind pages and pages, particularly on municipal power in America, a marvelous land where nothing is eternal, where what's no good is immediately replaced by something better. He had been especially taken with the fact that in many municipal organizations the president was simply a manager, elected and paid to increase the collective wealth, and, like the manager of any business, if he couldn't give an account of what he'd done with the money he was dismissed and replaced with someone more competent . . .

For days, Maria da Graça marveled at the portrait of her father's personality that was being revealed and even Sr. Américo Fonseca ended up appreciating this picture, confessing his ignorance of someone whose best and most intimate friend he'd always considered himself to be. In fact, preoccupied as he was with getting a piece of that pie, he had been very busy publicly proclaiming himself the trustee of the deceased, the loyal repository of his last wishes, the executor, to the letter, of all his provisos, though in private with Graça he simply called himself a friend of the family, an ad hoc secretary of an heiress who is as beautiful as she is happy, lucky is the one who unites in her bosom the full lineage of my sorely missed friend. But he had to cool his raptures in the face of Gracinha's very gentle but firm orders, no need to hurry, there were still many things to resolve before that, Sr. Fonseca should first concern himself with finding the homes of the various legatees, and he should especially not neglect to make a bit more of an effort in his search for Adélia. And in the afternoons when Sr. Fonseca returned to give an account of his search, tired of running around Monte, Chã de Cemitério, and Monte Sossego, having even once gone so far as the wilds of Craquinha, Graça, without even raising her eyes from her father's papers, only said, Don't give up, keep looking, she can't have vanished into thin air. But neither Sr. Fonseca on the street nor Graça among the papers ever found Adélia's trail.

*J*n despair over Sr. Fonseca's successive failures, Maria da Graça took it upon herself to find Adélia, shouldering the task with such determination that at the end of the first and only day that she devoted to a thorough search she was obliged to soak her aching and blistered feet in warm water. She had decided to verify Sr. Fonseca's itinerary so she followed his trail until she got to an Adélia in Chã de Cemitério who declared that she simply couldn't understand why they were so anxious to find someone just to give them a book. And with peals of laughter from her toothless mouth, she said that if she were Graça's age with her cute little face, she'd be at home right now enjoying the company of a man instead of searching in this heat for a dead person. Graça also smiled and asked how she knew Adélia was already dead if she didn't even know her. If no one in this town knows her it's because she's dead, she responded, and she said that when she was young she'd been skinny with wide, almond-shaped eyes, but had she known Sr. Napumoceno it wasn't a book that he would have gone and left her.

With her feet still in hot water it occurred to Graça that no one had remembered to ask if by chance Dona Eduarda had some information that might lead to Adélia. And so she called for her and when Dona Eduarda appeared in the doorway, smiling and asking if Miss Graça needed anything, Graça, also smiling, said that she needed to know who Adélia was because she wanted to give her a gift that Dona Eduarda's employer had left her. But Dona Eduarda didn't know and had never heard talk of any Adélia known to Sr. Napumoceno. Although, now that she recalled, she had, in fact, once found a piece of paper on the floor with that name on it, but the name was written so many times, sometimes in capital letters, sometimes in lower case, from the top to bottom of the page, that she thought the deceased was trying out his pen, especially because in several places the paper was torn by the nib of the pen. And because it was only that name that was written and nothing else and she didn't know anyone by that name, she'd thrown the piece of paper away, it hadn't seemed important.

As a last resort, Graça sounded out her mother to find out about other women in Sr. Napumoceno's life. Dona Chica had obstinately refused to move to Alto Mira-Mar and no argument on her daughter's part could convince her. She was well aware that only bodily matters had linked her to the father of her daughter, it was never anything more than satisfying a need, even though it was true that you could never say which child was born of love, and which of the simple vices of the body, since they were all made the same way. In the meantime she resisted leaving Lombo de Tanque, making the irrefutable argument that in Alto Mira-Mar she didn't know anyone who would fan her or give her sugar water the day she had another conniption. Graça provisionally accepted her mother's excuses but she remained split between Alto Mira-Mar and Lombo de Tanque because Dona Chica only accepted her daughter's move on condition that she visit every day. So when she got to her mother's house she confessed she was tired of walking from one end to the other of the city looking for an Adélia whom no one seemed to know. Dona Chica didn't react to the name, it seemed to Graça that it was entirely unknown to her and so, almost abruptly, she asked her if either before or after she'd known of other women in his life. No, never! replied Dona Chica curtly and adamantly, her eyes wide as if waiting for a painful revelation. Graça understood, almost by instinct, that she'd shocked the old woman, who, though wrinkled and already fat, had, in the end, believed herself to be the only woman in Sr. Napumoceno's life, and she felt sorry for her mother because she saw that after all a woman is the same at any age, and hugging her, she asked her, smiling, Mother, did you like him? And she was surprised at the heat she saw flare in those extinguished eyes, I liked him from the first because he was an attentive and friendly gentleman. I think that no one expected that what happened would happen, but the truth is things happened because I wanted them to. But neither before nor after did he have other women.

Graça didn't dare to contradict her mother, why destroy that illusion? She simply asked her if he'd had other cleaning ladies after she'd left and Dona Chica answered that she'd heard of several, but always short-term, until he'd unearthed Dona Eduarda. Graça then explained that he'd left presents for certain people, among them an Adélia whom Nho Fonseca was having trouble finding. But the name Adélia left Dona Chica

unperturbed. Adélia? No, no she didn't know her, didn't know
who she was. Probably some childhood friend.

So Maria da Graça decided to seek out Carlos. They'd met
in the presence of Sr. Fonseca, but it was a very formal meeting, a simple transfer of property, though in the end he'd been
rather nice, if there's anything you need clarified just call, I'm at
your disposal. After all, in the end, I liked the old man, though
he was stubborn and a little nuts. Especially in his old age.
Take that 387-page-long will! The devil wouldn't dream up
something like that! Graça smiled, and she placed her hand
on Carlos's arm: I know why he disinherited you! He left it
written down among some papers in a leather briefcase. It
was a joke I played on him, he answered. I swear it was a joke
and it never occurred to me that he'd get so mad, especially
because he knew what was said of him. I just wanted to
mess with him a little because he didn't do anything, and he
wouldn't let me work, always monkeying around with those
little gadgets, Come in, wait, busy! Graça smiled listening to
Carlos and they'd parted almost friends, even if Carlos was still
brooding over the legacy of that old house in Mato Inglês. But
he'd made a point of explaining to Graça. So that you don't
think I tried to put myself forward, it wasn't my idea to come
here. I was summoned! Of course I would have come the moment I knew, that's the truth, especially because I always hoped
he'd see that it was just a prank. But I was already in the office
when Dona Eduarda called me, Sr. Carlinhos . . . That's
what she calls me! Sr. Carlinhos, something terrible has happened! What? What's wrong! It's Sr. Araújo, the poor man!
And I heard her crying and I dropped the phone and I ran out,
a taxi happened to be passing so I was there in no time at all. I

told the driver to wait, but my uncle was already cold. I saw right away that he'd died at dawn. To die alone in that big house . . . Carlos stopped, and Graça felt his voice fade in anguish, but just for a second, then he quickly composed himself, formal once again.

When Sr. Fonseca got back from City Hall, where, will in hand, he'd gone to add the surname Araújo to the name Maria da Graça, Graça asked him to contact Carlos because she needed to talk to him. Always of service, Sr. Fonseca said that he would relay that Miss Graça Araújo asked Sr. Carlos Araújo to please be so kind as to give her a call. Now you need to try out your name, he said. It's a pretty name and it suits you. Graça promised to try it out a few times at home. Sr. Fonseca had taken charge of all the routine work related to the inheritance and he could account for everything, with the exception of Adélia, of whom he could find not even a trace, much less a flesh-and-blood person. He even went so far as to suggest that perhaps the deceased had been mistaken about the name. But Graça pooh-poohed such a notion; she told him that there are some names you never forget, much less get wrong. And he agreed with her right away and took this opportunity to say that he hoped he wouldn't be considered impertinent, he knew Graça had no need to sell any of the estate, fortunately there was more than enough for her to live on in peace, but he, Américo, had always loved the little house that the deceased possessed near Matiota and so, if it were possible, he'd very much like to buy it, obviously only if Miss Graça did not yet have another destiny in mind for it. Graça smiled. When it's all over we'll see what can be done, she said, and Sr. Fonseca left, happy, in search of Carlos.

Carlos arrived after 6:00 that evening, with a solemn and distant air. But Graça greeted him with two kisses, called him cousin and pushed him into the living room. I'm in a bit of a hurry, he began by saying, but she looked at him, and said with gravity, I'm in a terrible bind and I really need your help, so he immediately placed himself at her disposal, You already know I'm here for whatever you need, and he sat down and she smiled at him, I knew I could count on you. It seems that that man whom I still can't call *father* really liked music, but he still used a gramophone and I don't know how it works. Carlos smiled: It took a lot to satisfy his last wish. I don't know if I ever told you that that letter was on top of his desk, sealed but addressed to no one. I opened it but it said only: *I hope to be accompanied by the sound of Beethoven's funeral march.* At first I didn't worry about it, I thought it was well known. But in the end . . . You don't even know how lucky you were to be a daughter only afterward! No one has shown up yet to give you their heartfelt sympathies? For now, only Sr. Fonseca, Graça replied laughing. But it was a mixture of condolences and congratulations. But tell me something. Do you know anything about an Adélia? Adélia? Carlos said puzzled. I don't know if I know anyone with that name! Who is it? Adélia, Graça said very seriously, is someone who was the grand passion of that little man. No, I shouldn't say little man, the poor thing. But I still can't think of him as my father. You'll get used to it, Carlos smiled. To me it always seems forced for someone to call a man *father* whom they've known only as an adult. But you'll get used to it. In the meantime, keep calling him the deceased. . . . But Adélia . . . I've got it! Of course I know who it is! Me and everyone else obviously. What don't you end up knowing in S. Vicente! Like you, for instance! For a long time everyone knew he had a daughter, or rather that you were his daughter. But since you weren't actually registered people only whispered about it. When he began to go to see you at the high school people kept saying he wanted to register you as his daughter, but that your adoptive father already had. So you see it wasn't really a surprise to anyone. And here he thought he was making a revelation, said Graça. Well, in any case that story of registering you isn't true. Yes, but there's always a glimmer of truth. It's like the story of Adélia. He thought he was revealing something to you when the truth is that it was public knowledge that he even wanted to marry her. Everyone felt sorry for him, such a serious man, so circumspect, losing his head for a girl who wasn't even pretty. She was skinny, bony, and I remember her eyes always made her look frightened. You know how it is: those people who when they're frightened open their eyes wide. At the time all I heard was gossip. That he was head over heels in love, that he even wanted to marry the girl. But she had a boyfriend abroad and he returned and they told him things. It seems that Uncle would pick her up in his car and take her to Ribeira de Julião. At the time she must have been 22, and he was pushing 60. But he acted like a kid. He became a happy man for quite a while, something he'd never been before. I'd meet with him in the office and I'd see how he smiled and even whistled. Once I even found him singing a *morna*. No question, he was happy. I think he thought that no one knew anything and he even said that when he passed with her in the car he'd speed up so people couldn't tell who was inside. But you know how this place is; the minute you let out a fart, everyone smells it. So when her man came back there was such a scandal that he had to take refuge in S. Nicolau. Because everyone knew that the guy wanted to challenge him to a duel in the street, etc. It had been more than thirty years since he'd been to S. Nicolau, but he put out to sea to get away from his tormentor. People even tell funny stories about it. For example, they said that the guy, when he found out about their outings, didn't even want to talk with his Adélia about it, he went to look for Uncle straight-away. He didn't find him and so he called Adélia, I know about your outings with that Sr. Araújo. Tell me what you guys were doing together. She replied: Why don't you ask the person who told you about us what he and I were doing together. They say that you slept together. That's a big fat lie! We never slept to-gether! But you went out in his car with him? Yes, that I did, but we never slept together! Then what were you doing to-gether, the boy yelled, and she replied, Everything you do when you're awake! Graça laughed and asked Carlos if he'd ever met the couple. No, I never saw them together. The old man was very circumspect and jealous of his privacy. He was even convinced that the story only became known many years after it took place. I'm asking, Graça said, because he paints a different picture. He doesn't say, for instance, that he fled to S. Nicolau in fear. He says that he went in search of peace. Though it does come out that losing Adélia was difficult for him. I don't know anything about it, said Carlos. What I know is what was said. Especially because it seems like the guy left and no one ever said anything about Adélia and the old man again. Probably the fright cured him of his passion. But it seems that with the cure he also lost his cheerfulness. Because I remember that when I met him, I was a kid and he was a warm-hearted man who liked to play with me, etc. But everyone says that he suddenly became moody, quiet, he hardly smiled and he often seemed moonstruck. The truth is that his personality changed completely. Even the way he dressed! You saw that rag of a suit! I do know that I remember him as a dandy, always well-dressed, well-shod, and well-coiffed. It was little by little that he began to let himself go, until he got to the point of not having a suit to be buried in. You know why, Graça began to say, but Carlos cut her short saying that such an explanation could only come from a madman. Come on, cousin, who's ever heard of keeping a suit in the pantry? Let's go back to our Adélia then, Graça pleaded. That's who I need to know about. You said she was ugly, but what's clear is that our man liked her, and even left her a book, probably as a memento. *Alone*, by António Nobre. That's a good one! Carlos exclaimed and burst out laughing. What remains to be seen is if she knows how to read. The truth is I never heard anything more about her. The guy went away and I remember that a little while later I saw her and she was knocked up. Pregnant, you mean, Graça corrected. Yes, pregnant. Then I never saw her again. That's too bad, Graça said. I'd very much like to meet her to find out what the woman was like who inspired such a grand passion in the old man. Well, what I know for sure, Carlos said laughing, is that meeting her 20 years later you wouldn't understand how it was possible for him to have fallen for the fat ass you'd find. Because a hard life and children ruin our women and at 50 they're already wrecks. Adélia might even be one of those people who makes her living begging door to door. Because there's no other explanation for no one knowing anything about her. Patience, Graça smiled. Let's keep hoping that something will come to light. Tell me, would you like to trade the old house in Mato Inglês for the house in Matiota? Carlos looked at her and said what he'd like is for her to offer him a drink. Graça got up and started searching as Carlos said that the old man always had good aged *aguardente* from Santo Antão. He aged it himself in an oak barrel. Four years, imagine that! Sometimes, after he considered me to be of age, he allowed me the honor of drinking with him.

While she was pouring the drinks Graça asked why Carlos didn't accept the trade, if it was true that he didn't need the old house. For the simple reason that it wasn't the old guy's wish, Carlos replied smiling, and it could easily happen that, pissed off about the swap, he'd come at night to drag me out of bed by my heels. Besides, he added more seriously, everyone already knows that the house in Matiota will go to Sr. Fonseca. Sr. Fonseca? Graça exclaimed. Why Sr. Fonseca? Well, Carlos said taking a sip, all of S. Vicente says that Sr. Fonseca is your errand boy because of the house in Matiota. But it was only a moment ago that he spoke to me about selling him that house and I didn't say Yes because I was thinking of you. Because the truth is he's never shown any interest in anything whatsoever. Carlos continued to drink his liqueur. Then he said that most likely Sr. Fonseca had never spoken to anyone about the house, but people in S. Vicente are like that: they guess people's thoughts. We may still be unsure what we're thinking but they already know. Often you hear things about yourself that you'd never thought of before and they end up happening in the end. In any case, he'll be well served because it's a good house. Do you remember the will? Until my daughter Maria da Graça takes effective possession of my worldly goods, twice a week, on Tuesdays and Fridays, my housekeeper, Dona Eduarda, will go to Matiota to clean and air out the house. Graça didn't laugh while Carlos cited this passage from the will. And for a moment they were silent while she thought about the order the old man had imposed on the disbursement of his things after death: every Saturday the sum of 100 *escudos* will be distributed among the poor who come to knock at my door in alms of one *escudo* and two *escudos* and fifty *centavos*. However, if any is left over, the same will be distributed on other days of the week; on the 30th of each month Maria da Graça will send the sum of 300 *escudos* to the attached list of people in S. Nicolau. This amount should be sent as a money order since that's the fastest and most secure means; don't forget to have my Olivetti typewriter oiled from time to time. It's an excellent machine and if it's well cared for it will last for many more years and will continue to be of service; I hope that my grave will be marked with a simple stone, of marble, on which only the following will be inscribed: *Napumoceno da Silva Araújo 1898–19 . . , Lived and Died with Dignity*. I will leave separate instructions for the funerary music . . . Carlos, Graça said suddenly, tell me about him. What kind of man was he? Carlos looked at her but remained silent for a while. To be honest, I don't know what to tell you, he said finally. I think I never thought about it. But now I think that above all else he was a man who was swept up in events. He landed barefoot in S. Vicente and only bought real shoes when he became rich. But I think he himself never knew how or why he did, even if it's true that he was smart and had incredible luck. But I think he was always afraid of becoming the Napumoceno of S. Nicolau again. And that's why he was so anxious, and a little

wary, and took offense so easily. Carlos, Graça asked again, did
he like you a lot? Carlos smiled. At first I thought he didn't like
me very much, probably because I didn't like him much. So
when he sent me to school and I failed there was hell to
pay. But until then he'd taken me everywhere and it was, my
nephew this, my nephew that. He was very demanding, he
wanted, imagine this, for me to be the best student in the high
school, for me to have the highest grades. He said that I had to
be a man and that only books, only school, made men. And
then he became disillusioned with me and stopped holding my
hand and called me only *young man*. Come here, young man!
What you want is to be a donkey, right? Well than I'll get you a
straw packsaddle. That's when he still asked me about my
grades. The last time I flunked out he simply said: Oh well, you
can lead a horse to water, but you can't make him drink. So,
from now on you're going to work, earn your keep by the sweat
of your brow. And he found me a job. But a little while later he
changed toward me again, because once, after I'd already been
out of school for a while, he introduced me to Dr. Sousa, his
great friend, I don't know if you know about him, and he introduced me as his nephew, something he hadn't called me in a
long time. And then there was that Christmas when it was
only the four of us with Chinese porcelain and crystal glasses
and after it was over he patted me on the back and said that I'd
done well, that he was pleased with me. And at the beginning
of the new year I started to work at Araújo, Ltd.

Graça was distracted as she listened to Carlos and when he
finished his drink and got up to go she said to him, one of
these weekends why don't the two of us go look for Adélia, and
he nodded and left. Graça remained seated, thinking of a way

to find out if the Adélia she'd met wasn't her father's Adélia, when Dona Eduarda came in and interrupted her thoughts to ask her if she needed anything. And since Graça said that she didn't need anything, that she was fine, she took the opportunity to ask how things were going. Dona Eduarda knew that she was named in the will for a specific legacy and had already told her that if possible she'd like to receive it as a lump sum. She wanted to live out her old age raising chickens. Chickens had always been her weakness and what she most wanted in the world was a small backyard where she could have her little animals. Nothing gives me more pleasure than to be awakened by a rooster, she said smiling broadly. And also having fresh eggs at home. Sr. Araújo loved poached eggs. Actually what he liked most were cucumbers and poached eggs. She, Eduarda had told him many times: Sr. Araújo, watch out, too many eggs isn't good for you and cucumber is hard to digest. But he'd reply: There are no indigestible foods, woman! People are the ones who are hard to digest, especially women! And so I said, Sr. Araújo, please excuse my being so forward, but I am also a woman. And he smiled, and said, you, Eduarda, are not a woman, you are the younger mother I found. But don't worry because you won't be the worse for it. I've already provided for you in my will. I didn't say anything and he asked if that didn't make me happy and so I said that I didn't understand what he'd said. So then he explained that my name was in his will as a beneficiary. My goodness, man, you say such things. God will give you life and health to enjoy what is yours, but he said, No, Eduarda, I already feel old and full of holes inside. And he would get up from his canvas chair and walk up and down the living room a bit, and then go back to his chair, and I would

tell him that it was the cucumber, the cucumber and the eggs
you eat too much of! But he'd say, what cucumber, this is age,
and age forgives no one. He lasted a few more years, but was
always sickly, with one thing or another. He complained of
rheumatism, and at the end I had to rub oil into his calves, his
knees, almost every day, he didn't like medicines, he said that
when he was young he'd taken enough. But once he had the
beginnings of pneumonia, and I had to call the doctor to the
house, and he gave him some medicines with strange names,
something biotic . . . Antibiotic? . . . Yes, that might be it,
but the fact is that after that he didn't hear well, he always said
that it was because of those damned medicines they'd put in
his body, and one day I even said to him why don't you put one
of those things in your ear that help people hear better, the
priest has one and now he no longer has any complaints about
his hearing, but he said right away, God keep me from having
to use a thing like that! I'd rather die deaf! But then, perhaps
because he was always sitting and reading—thank God he always had his eyesight, and a good thing too, because he no
longer left the house, sometimes he'd spend whole days without even going out to the porch that he liked so much, sitting
in his pajamas at home in that canvas chair, reading or writing—he ended up suffering from constipation. Once two
weeks went by without him going to the bathroom and I noticed without his needing to say anything, until one day I said,
Sr. Araújo, please forgive my being so forward but I think you
should take something to relieve your body, those things kept
inside aren't good for us, but he just shrugged his shoulders and
said, What's to be done about it? And so I made a wild herb
tea and put a lot of garlic in his food, luckily he liked garlic,

and I also made a liqueur syrup with honey, garlic, lemon, a bit of mint, and bay leaves, and he did indeed get better and from then on he went to the bathroom at least every other day, but one day he said, It's been a long time since I've seen myself in the mirror and today I noticed that I've aged a lot, and I said, You know sir you should make an effort to shave at least once a week, that way at least you'd see your face in the mirror. But after the time I found him with his face covered in cuts, I told him I would give him a shave. He protested, of course, You already think I'm some sort of invalid! But the truth is that he had to go along with it because he already trembled too much and would cut himself all over. Luckily, his beard was just on his chin and I would give him a shave every other day and I would even joke with him saying that In your beard you took after your mother and he said, Thank goodness for that because otherwise it would be a disaster. By then even just for him to read I had to place a pillow on his lap when he was seated in the canvas chair because he couldn't hold the book straight, it would keep slipping from his hands.

Dona Eduarda told her story and cried, large tears running down her face, but she continued to speak as if she were two people, one who was crying and one who was telling a story, and in looking at her Graça would wring her hands and bite her lip, but finally a *poor man* escaped her, which made Dona Eduarda sob while she talked about how he began to have trouble eating because, due to the tremor he had, he'd often miss his mouth and sometimes he would aim the spoon with gestures that he meant to be quick, but he'd miss, and the spoon would hit his Adam's apple, a sharp little Adam's apple he had, only he could have had an Adam's apple like that, and with age it became even sharper, but then the spoon would hit him in the chin, when it was fork-food there wasn't much of a problem, but when it was soup he would get all dirty and so then Dona Eduarda began to wrap a napkin around his neck and he no longer objected, even though he'd had to abandon eating with a fork because the fork was more dangerous when he missed his mouth, as happened once when he pricked his chin and said, Shit, damn this dog's life! And him such an educated man! And he picked up his plate and got up with the pricks from the fork still visible on his chin and Dona Eduarda swore she saw tears in the eyes of that man and she too felt something inside and she even said, Leave it I'll stay and feed you, but he let out a cry, opened his eyes wide and said, Better dead than in that state! But then he came to his senses and said, My goodness, what is this, I don't know where this tremor comes from, this is no longer living, and I said, It's God's will, you have to be patient, but he said, It's our sins that we pay for and I'm paying! And in fact many times he'd choke on the food in his mouth, probably just when he was about to swallow, and once when he'd choked on the food that he'd just chewed it all came out and dirtied the table and the plate and the floor, and he had such a severe coughing fit that his eyes welled up and so from then on I only gave him soft food, almost mush, even the meat I would chop very fine so that he could swallow it without difficulty, though it's true that he preferred fish, he was always a man for a good deep-sea fish and he'd always liked to pick it out for himself at the market.

Dona Eduarda dried her tears, Graça sniffled and wanted to tell her to be quiet, to say no more, but she couldn't get the words out, and she stood before Dona Eduarda, wanting to choke on her words, reliving that long and infinitely painful suffering that she was re-creating, thinking, why didn't you call me to help you? And while Dona Eduarda recounted one story after another in a quiet voice, she saw her father at the table with the spoon in his hand trying to hit his mouth and saw his eyes filled with tears because of the coughing and lived that impotence in the face of the suffering of old age while Dona Eduarda related how often she would say, Sir, you should go out a little, get a little sun, visit your friends, it would do you good, you need to get another suit for your outings, the suit that's here has no wear left in it, what an idea to hang it in the pantry, only you sir, would do something like that, of course if I'd been here, he wouldn't have done it, out of the question, but, you know, he'd sent me home, You, Eduarda, you've never had a vacation in your life, take advantage of these few days, go to Santo Antão, and when you return I'll call you, and so it was that the day of his departure for S. Nicolau, he was at home alone, though it's true that I went over everything before I left, but, in the end, what I know for sure is that he refused to have another suit made, even though I told him Look, there's life and there's death, sir, you may need it at any time, but he would say he no longer needed clothes.

Graça asked herself how it was that, in the midst of all that suffering, he had remembered the funeral march for the burial and asked Dona Eduarda if he still wrote during that last period of his life. Dona Eduarda said that as for writing he no longer wrote because of the tremor. He simply read and the last thing she remembered seeing him write was that letter that Master Carlos had found on top of the desk. In any case, she knew about it because he'd told her a long time ago that in the event of his death the first thing to do was to open that letter. But as for writing, he hadn't written in a long time, he simply read and sometimes he asked her to wind the gramophone and put on the record with a coronet on the cover and he would lie still in his chair, his eyes open as if he were dead, and once I even thought he'd felt something and I was frightened and said, Sr. Araújo, Sr. Araújo, what's wrong? But he was spooked by my scream and scolded me, even though that music really does seem like funeral music, but one day he fell asleep in the chair, in any case it was usual for him to have his nap in the canvas chair and I always came in without making noise so as not to wake him, and one day I came in and he was smiling, but then I saw that he was sleeping and smiling, he was probably dreaming, he heard me come in and said, Put on that record, you know the one, and while I was doing that I said, I thought you were sleeping, but he kept smiling and began to say a few words that I didn't quite understand but it was as if he was talking to someone, as if he was saying to her, Stop it, stop horsing around! But at one point he said, Watch out for the door Adélia! But then he woke up and said I must have been dreaming but he stayed in that half-sleep and the following morning I came into the room to open the window and he didn't say Good morning as he usually did, and I thought that maybe he was still sleeping and only when I opened the window did I see that he was sleeping the sleep of angels.